Ash

MALINDA LO

*Hodder
Children's
Books*

HODDER CHILDREN'S BOOKS

First published in the USA in 2009 by Little Brown & Company
First published in Great Britain in 2010 by Hodder Children's Books
This edition published in 2016 by Hodder and Stoughton

16

Text copyright © Malinda Lo, 2009

The moral right of the author has been asserted.

A CIP catalogue record for this book is available from the British Library

ISBN-13: 978 0 340 98837 4

Typeset in Bembo by Avon DataSet Ltd, Bidford-on-Avon, Warwickshire

Printed and bound in Great Britain by Clays Ltd, St Ives plc

The paper and board used in this book are made from wood
from responsible sources.

MIX
Paper from
responsible sources
FSC® C104740

Hodder Children's Books
An imprint of Hachette Children's Group
Part of Hodder and Stoughton
Carmelite House
50 Victoria Embankment
London EC4Y 0DZ

An Hachette UK Company
www.hachette.co.uk

www.hachettechildrens.co.uk

In memory of my grandmother,
Ruth Earnshaw Lo
(1910–2006)

Part One

The Fairy

1

Aisling's mother died at midsummer. She had fallen sick so suddenly that some of the villagers wondered if the fairies had come and taken her, for she was still young and beautiful. She was buried three days later beneath the hawthorn tree behind the house, just as twilight was darkening the sky.

Maire Solanya, the village greenwitch, came that evening to perform the old rituals over the grave. She stood at the foot of the mound of black soil, a thin old woman with white hair bound in a braid that reached her hips, her face a finely drawn map of lines. Aisling and her father stood across from each other on either side of the grave, and at the head of it, resting on the simple headstone, was the burning candle. Aisling's father had lit it shortly after Elinor died, and it would burn all night, sheltered by the curving glass around it. The gravestone was a plain piece of slate carved with her name: Elinor. Grass and tree roots would grow up around it as the months and years passed, until it would seem as if it had always been there.

Maire Solanya said in her low, clear voice, 'From life to life, from breath to breath, we remember Elinor.' She held a round loaf of bread in her hands, and she tore off a small piece and ate it, chewing deliberately, before handing the loaf to Aisling's father. He pulled off his own piece, then passed it to his daughter. It was still warm, and it smelled like her mother's kitchen after baking. But it hadn't come from her mother's hands, and that realization made a hard lump rise in her throat. The bread was tasteless.

Maire Solanya took the loaf from her, its crust gaping open, and placed it on the gravestone next to the candle. Aisling couldn't shake the feeling that her mother had merely gone out on an errand and would come home at any moment and wonder what the three of them were doing. It didn't seem possible that she was buried there, at the foot of the hawthorn tree, in the ground. She had seen her mother's body after she died, of course, but her face had lost all of the vibrancy that made her recognizable. And it was easier to believe the village rumours than to sit with the ache inside herself.

She remembered those rumours now, while she stood with her father and Maire Solanya in a tense silence, waiting as the sun set over the Wood. Everyone had always said that Elinor had some magic in her, and everyone knew that fairies – if they existed – were drawn to that. So Aisling's father had ordered all the old rituals, even though he did not believe in them, just in case. She was not entirely sure what she herself believed, but she knew that her mother would want them to do these rituals for her, and that was enough.

When the sun slipped below the horizon, the greenwitch said, 'Sleep in peace, Elinor,' and scattered a gold powder over the grave to bind Elinor to the earth. On the freshly turned soil, the gold glittered like fairy dust.

Aisling's father stepped around the grave and put a hand on her shoulder. 'Go back to the house, Ash.' He had told her that he would keep vigil over the grave all night. Some said that the Fairy Hunt sought out souls on the night after burial, and only those who were guarded by their loved ones would be left to rest in peace.

She walked slowly up the hill back to the house. When she turned at the kitchen door to look down towards the garden, Maire Solanya was making three circles around the grave before she left. Just beyond the hawthorn tree, the Wood was dark and silent. The single candle glimmered, and Ash could see the shape of her father as he knelt beside the grave.

The housekeeper, Anya, came out the kitchen door and caressed Ash's hair. 'It will be all right,' Anya said. 'Come inside before night falls. Your mother's spirit will be safe with your father watching over her.'

★ ★ ★

3

Ash woke in the middle of the night from a dream of horses – tall, thundering white horses with foaming mouths and slender, wraith-like riders. She swung her legs over the side of the bed and went to the window that looked out over the Wood. She searched for the light of the candle by the grave but saw only darkness. Then there was movement at the edge of the trees, and she shivered. Where was her father?

She ran down the stairs, through the kitchen, and out of the back door. The wind was rising. She ran down the hillside in her bare feet, feeling the earth alive beneath her toes, her nightgown flying behind her in white linen wings. She ran past the garden's rows of carrots and cabbages and towards the dark, hulking line of the Wood. Beneath the hawthorn tree, the glass cover was tipped over on its side, the candle was snuffed out, and her father was gone. She knelt on the ground and reached for the candle, but she hadn't brought matches and could not light it.

The wind gusted over her, whipping her hair around her face. The dark pressed against her, and she wondered if her father had given up his vigil because of the weight of the night on his back. She heard the hoofbeats then, coming closer and closer. She thought she saw a faint glimmer of white in the dark Wood, a glow of otherworldly light, like stardust caught behind glass. She was frightened, but she would not leave her mother. She lay down on the grave, pressing her body into the warm earth and her cheek against the gravestone. The hooves came closer, and she heard the high, thin sound of a bugle. The wind rushed towards her, and the cries of the riders were clear upon the air: They called for her mother, for Elinor. The ground beneath Ash's body heaved, and she let out a scream of fright as she felt the world buckle beneath her, earth and stone and moss and root twisting up as if it were clawed by a mighty hand. There was a roaring sound in her ears as the horses surrounded her, and she squeezed her eyes shut, afraid of what she might see. She dug her fingers into the ground, clinging to the earth where her mother lay buried.

And then there was a sudden silence, and in that silence she could hear the breathing of horses, the heaving of their lungs, the musical jingle of bit and bridle, and the whisper of voices like silvery bells. She thought she heard someone say, 'She is only a child. Let her go.'

The wind roared again, so fierce that she thought she would be pulled from the ground and thrown aside like a rag doll, but when it died down the horses were gone, and the night was quiet. The air hummed as it did after a storm. When she opened her eyes, the ground all around her was marked with hoofprints.

Ash woke up suddenly in her own bed, her heart pounding. She sat up, gasping for breath as though she were being suffocated, and saw the early morning light coming through the curtains. She ran to the window and looked out; her father was coming slowly up the hill. When she heard him come into the house and close the kitchen door, she realized she had been gripping the windowsill with white fingers. She let go, feeling foolish. But just as she began to turn away, she saw something gleaming on the windowsill: in the spaces where the paint had cracked, gold dust glittered.

2

In that country, the great expanse of the Wood descends from the Northern Mountains foothills of blue pine, sweeping south towards the more civilized oak and birch of the King's Forest. No one travels into the interior of the Wood, although it must once have been populated, because numerous roads and tracks lead into it. Those tracks have long been abandoned, and the Wood is thought to be the home of dangerous beasts and the most powerful of all the fairies. Some scholars speculate that once upon a time, the country was thick with magic; in addition to fairies there were powerful sorcerers and witches who did more than brew willow bark tea to calm a child's fever.

But as time passed, the magic faded, leaving behind only a faint memory of its power. Some said there was a great war that drove away the sorcerers and lasted for so many years that the very shape of the land changed: Mountains became valleys beneath the tread of thousands of soldiers, and rivers were rerouted to make way for grand new palaces. But all that is merely conjecture; no history books survived to tell the tale. Only the greenwitches remained, and their magic was limited to saying the old rites for birth and marriage and death. Sometimes they brewed love potions for girls who hadn't met their lovers by Midsummer's Eve, and sometimes the love potions even worked. Usually that was enough to remind the people that magic still lurked in half-forgotten places.

But even if magic was so rare it was more like myth than reality, the people of that country still loved their fairy tales. They told stories about brownies, who helpfully did the chores overnight in exchange for a bowl of cream. There were boggarts, mischievous creatures who slammed doors and shattered pottery or pawed through a household's winter stores in search of sweets. There were handsome love-talkers, who seduced girls with their charm and wit and then left them to pine away for a love that could never be. Children were warned to stay away from strange flickering lights at midnight, for if a person once set foot inside a fairy ring, he would never be able to leave.

Most of the people of that country lived on the borders of the Wood in pine-board houses built up close to the trees, where the old magic lingered. South of the Wood the land sloped down in fertile, rich farmland towards the sea. The farmers, who lived in quaint stone cottages surrounded by broad fields, grew yellow squash and long green beans and bushels of wheat. In the very southern tip of the country they grew oranges and lemons, which were shipped north to the Royal City during harvest season to be made into lemonade and orange punch. The farmers didn't believe in Wood fairies, but they listened for the tread of field dwellers and hobgoblins, who could bless a crop or eat it all. They set out bowls of honey wine to tempt the fairies away from milking cows, and left out baskets of fruit to distract them from their orchards.

In a country so fond of its fairy stories, where the people clung to the memory of magic with a deep and hungry nostalgia, it was no surprise that philosophers and their church faced a difficult task when they landed in Seatown four generations ago. Legends began to spring up about the philosophers – that they were the sorcerers of old who had lost their magic; that they came from the hot desert places of the Far South, where illusions and spells abounded; that they once were royal advisors who had betrayed their rulers. But the philosophers themselves disliked this penchant for telling tales and insisted upon their own, much plainer history.

They reported that they were indeed from the south, from the empire of Concordia to be exact, and they had come north to spread the wisdom of their emperor. They built churches out of plaster and wood and sat within them, reading books written in foreign tongues.

They argued passionately with the village greenwitches, claiming that all those fairy tales were nothing but the stuff of nonsense – there were no greenies or goblins. Had anyone ever actually seen a brag or a dunter or a mermaid? Or were they only stories told to children at bedtime? The greenwitches grumbled in response, and some insisted that they *had* run into klippes at twilight, or seen sprites slipping among the shadows of the Wood at Midsummer.

Perhaps because philosophers tended to be men and greenwitches tended to be women, the argument took on an overly heated tone. Insults were hurled: The philosophers called the greenwitches superstitious old wives, and the greenwitches retorted that not one of them was married. The greenwitches derided the philosophers as joyless old men afraid of magic, and the philosophers, not surprisingly, protested that they found much joy in the *real* world. And then they brought out their largest tomes bound in gold, the leather covers stamped with the five-cornered star of the Concordian Empire, and threw open the heavy covers. They pointed to the unreadable text and said, 'Look! There is the real world. All our learning, all our experiences, written down fact by fact. There are no myths here; only facts. Fairies are mere fictions. We deal in the truth.'

The oldest, most powerful greenwitch at the time, a wise and wiry woman by the name of Maire Nicneva, laughed at those white-bearded men in their red-pointed caps and replied, 'You shall not discover the truth by being blinded to faith.'

From then on, for a period of at least two generations, philosophers had a hard time in that country. They continued to build their churches in village greens dotting the coast, but found it difficult to progress into the interior of the country. The closer they came to the Wood, the more angry the people became. They were called liars and unbelievers, and while they were never physically harmed, even children laughed at them – at their strange crimson costumes and heavy, dusty books locked in huge, iron-bound trunks. But one day the King met a philosopher who was less stubborn than the others, and they sat down together and talked about the smell of spring and the taste of the sweetest oranges, and they grew to like one another. The King even took the philosopher on a hunt, and as hunting is that people's favorite sport, all the country began to listen more seriously to the philosophers.

By that time the philosophers had also begun to change their approach to this people. Rather than insisting that there was no such thing as magic, they began to merely suggest that perhaps magic was not as prevalent as it once was. They asked, have you ever seen an elf? Or did you work hard on your own to build your house, to feed your children, to put clothes on your family's backs? And gradually the idea took root that magic was merely an old country superstition.

The people of Rook Hill, however, the small northern village where Aisling lived with her father, kept to the old ways. It was far enough from the Royal City to make the philosophy being preached by the King's many advisors seem stranger than the fairy tales most mothers told their children. Ash remembered playing in her mother's herb garden while listening to tales about brownies or picts or selkies. Sometimes the greenwitch Maire Solanya joined them, and she too told tales, though hers were darker. Once she told a story about a young woman who wandered for a month through the silver mines in the Northern Mountains, seeking her lost lover, only to find herself confronted by a family of knockers who demanded her first-born child in return for their help in finding him.

When Ash looked frightened, Maire Solanya said, 'Fear will teach you where to be careful.'

Her mother had been apprenticed to Maire Solanya when she was a girl, and sometimes she taught Ash the differences between various herbs that grew in her garden – feverfew for headache, meadowsweet for a burn – but when she married William, a merchant, she left her apprenticeship. Sometimes in the evenings after supper, they would argue about whether or not she should go back to that calling, and usually Ash remembered those conversations as friendly debates, but once her parents' voices took on harder tones. 'The King's chief philosopher himself has said that greenwitches do nothing more than calm one's nerves – which is no small thing,' William said. Ash had been sent up to bed, but she had come back downstairs to ask her mother a question, and when she heard her father's voice, she hesitated in the hall outside the parlour.

'Those philosophers only sit in their churches and issue judgements based on inaccurate texts from Concordia,' her mother said. 'They know nothing about what a greenwitch does.'

William sighed. 'They are not distant scholars, Elinor; they have studied your herbal practices in detail.'

'It is about more than herbal practices,' she countered. 'You know that.'

'Are you saying that all those tales you tell Ash have any basis in reality?' he said in disbelief. 'They are only bedtime stories – it is superstition, nothing more.'

Elinor's voice took on an edge that Ash had never heard before. 'Those tales serve a purpose, William, and how dare you dismiss our traditions as superstition? There is a reason they have survived.'

'It will do you and our daughter no good to align yourselves with the past,' William said, sounding frustrated. 'The King does not follow those ways anymore, and you must understand that keeping to those traditions will only harm my standing in court.'

Her mother said curtly, 'I won't abandon the truth, William, and I won't lie about it, either.'

There was a sharp silence after that, and Ash retreated

13

back upstairs, her question forgotten. It was unsettling to hear them argue; she had never before realized the depth of their disagreement. But the next morning there was no trace of the argument in her parents' faces. In the months that followed, Ash listened a bit anxiously whenever her parents' conversation began to turn in that direction, but she never heard them bring it up again. When her mother fell sick so suddenly, her father called Maire Solanya to attend her, and Ash knew it was because he loved Elinor more than his beliefs.

Two weeks after her mother's funeral, Ash's father left for the Royal City. At breakfast that morning, she asked him, 'When will you come back?'

'Possibly not until autumn,' he said. Before her mother died, her father would leave them for months at a time to do business in the south. When he returned he would bring back gifts: slippery, shiny silks, or thick woollen tweeds, or toy dolls made of pale, cold porcelain.

'Did Mother ever go with you?' she asked, and he seemed surprised by her question.

'She did travel with me to Seatown once,' he answered, 'but she did not like it. She said she missed the Wood.' He suddenly looked deeply sad, and he rubbed his hand over his face as if he were brushing away the memories. 'She did like visiting the booksellers' bazaar, though. She'd spend hours there while I worked.'

Ash asked, 'Will you bring me a new book, Father?'

He seemed taken aback, but then he said gruffly, 'I suppose you are your mother's daughter.' He reached out and ruffled her hair, and he let his hand linger, warm and firm, on her forehead.

After breakfast, Ash sat on the front steps and watched her father and his driver loading trunks onto the carriage. It was a week's journey from Rook Hill to the Royal City, barring any mishaps. When they were ready to depart, he came over to Ash. She stood up, and he put a hand on her shoulder and said, 'Be a good girl and listen to Anya. I'll send news when I can.'

'Yes, Father,' she replied, and looked down at the ground, staring at the toes of his polished black boots.

He lifted her chin in his hand and said, 'Don't spend too much time daydreaming. You're a big girl now.' He touched her cheek and then turned to go to the carriage. She watched as it pulled away, and she stood on the steps long after it had gone out of sight, around the bend.

After her father left for the City, she went down to the grave every day, usually at twilight. The letters carved into the headstone spelling out her mother's name were sharp and fresh, and the rectangle of earth that marked the length of the grave was still distinct, but even within a few weeks of the burial, wildflowers and grasses had begun to grow. Sitting with her back against the tree, she remembered a tale her mother had once told her about a fairy who lived in the mountains north of Rook Hill. This fairy was a shape-shifter, and a cruel one at that. If a family had just lost someone, this fairy would visit them, knocking on their door after sunset. When they opened the door, they would see their departed loved one standing there, as real as could be. It would be tempting to invite her in, for in the depths of grief, sometimes one cannot tell the difference between illusion and reality. But those who gave in had to pay a price, for to invite death inside would mean striking a bargain with it.

'What price did they have to pay?' Ash had asked her mother.

'Generally,' her mother responded, 'the fairies ask for the same thing: a family's first-born child, to take back with them to Taninli and mould into their own creature.'

'What sort of creature?' Ash asked curiously.

Her mother had been kneading dough that morning, and she paused in her work to look out of the kitchen window at the Wood. 'You know, I've never seen such a creature,' her mother said thoughtfully. 'It must be a strange one.' And then to dispel the dark mood, her mother laughed and said, 'It's nothing to worry about, my dear. Simply don't answer the door after sunset.'

And she reached over and caressed her daughter's cheek, leaving a light dusting of flour on her face.

★ ★ ★

The summer passed slowly. Her father sent news every few weeks, punctuating the warm stillness with reports from the south: There had been a storm on the road, and it had delayed them. When they arrived in the Royal City, a new King's Huntress had just been appointed, and there was a grand parade. In Seatown, her father had attended a ball at a grand estate on the cliffs. Ash and Anya read his letters together, and afterwards, Ash folded them between the pages of her mother's favourite book, a collection of fairy tales that had been read so often the cover had come loose.

One market day, Ash went with Anya into the village. While Anya finished her errands, Ash wandered among the peddler's stalls in the village green. Coming to a cart piled high with herbs, she buried her nose among them and inhaled. When she looked up, the greenwitch was standing beside the cart, watching her.

'Where is Anya?' Maire Solanya asked.

'She is at the candlemaker's,' Ash said.

'And your father? Has he sent news of when he will return?'

'No,' Ash answered. 'Why?'

But the greenwitch did not answer her question. Instead, she bent down to Ash's eye level and looked at her closely. The woman had strangely pale blue eyes and sharply arched grey eyebrows. 'Do you miss your mother?' she asked.

Ash stepped back, startled. 'Of course I miss her,' she said.

'You must let her go,' Maire Solanya said softly. Ash felt tears prick at the corners of her eyes. 'Your mother was a great woman,' the greenwitch continued. 'She is happy where she is now. You must not wish her back.'

Ash blinked, and the tears spilled over; she felt as if the greenwitch were tugging them out of her one by one.

Maire Solanya's features softened with compassion, and she reached out and brushed away the teardrops. Her fingertips were cool and dry. 'It will be all right,' she said gently. 'We will never forget her.'

By the time Anya came to collect her, she had stopped crying and was sitting on the stone bench at the edge of the green, and Maire Solanya had gone. They walked home silently, and though Anya asked her if she was upset, Ash only shook her head. At home a letter had been left for them, wedged into the edge of the front door, and Anya handed it to Ash as they went inside. While Anya put away the items she had purchased at the market, Ash unsealed the letter, spreading it out on the kitchen table. She read it twice, because the first time she had read it she could not believe it.

'What news?' Anya finally asked, coming to join her at the table.

'Father is coming back,' Ash said.

'Well, that's wonderful,' Anya said with a smile. 'Sooner than expected!'

'He is bringing someone with him,' Ash said. Something in her voice caused Anya to take the letter from her, puzzled, and read it herself. 'I am to have a stepmother, and two stepsisters,' Ash said. She was stunned. 'They will be here in two weeks.'

After the letter arrived, the days passed in a blur. Anya was busy preparing the house as William had instructed. Later, Ash could never remember if she had helped to clean her mother's things out of her parents' bedchamber, or if Anya had simply swept them all into a trunk and out of sight. But she did remember that on the morning of her father's scheduled return, she visited what had been her mother's room and stood on the thick gold-and-brown rug in a pool of sunlight coming through the leaded glass windows. The wardrobe was empty now, and the door was partway open, as if inviting Ash to look inside and make sure that all traces of her mother were gone.

It was late in the day when the carriage finally pulled into the courtyard. Ash went outside to meet them, and her new stepmother, Lady Isobel Quinn, looked at Ash with an expression hovering between resignation and impatience. As her new stepsisters climbed out of the carriage, Ana, who was twelve – 'just your age; she will make a wonderful playmate for you,' her father had written hopefully – complained of hunger. Clara, who was only ten, looked up at the house with wide, anxious eyes. Anya had told Ash to be polite to them, but all she could feel at the moment of their arrival was a thick, burning anger inside her. It licked at her belly when she heard her stepmother comment on the smallness of the staircase; it throbbed at her temples when Ana demanded that Ash's own room be given up for her; it roared inside her when her father reached for his new wife's hand and led her into her mother's room.

That night, while her father and stepmother and stepsisters sat together in the parlour, exclaiming over the gifts he had brought them from Seatown, Ash slipped away from them all. She skidded down the hill on feet made clumsy from suppressed emotion, and sank down on the ground beside her mother's grave, clutching her knees tight to her chest. All her frustration and sadness began to bubble up to the surface, sliding out of her in hot teardrops. She tried to not make a sound – she did not want anyone to hear her – but her body shook as she cried. When the tightness inside her finally relaxed, she lay down on the earth, her cheek pillowed on her hand, staring slackly at the faint outlines of her mother's tombstone in the dark.

She didn't see the man standing in the Wood beyond the house, watching her. He had white hair and eyes so blue they were like jewels, and he was dressed all in silvery white. The air around him seemed to crack in places, and his moonlight-coloured cloak wavered at those cracks as if he weren't quite all there. If Ash had seen him, she might have thought that he was a fairy, for all around him the Wood seemed enmeshed in a web of illusion. One moment the trees were solid as stone around him; the next it was as if he were standing among grand marble pillars in a magnificent palace. But Ash did not see him. She lay there in the dark, rubbing away her tears, and when she was too tired to cry any more, she turned over on to her back and fell asleep.

3

Her father had been back for nearly a week when Maire Solanya came to see him. Ash almost missed her visit entirely, because she had been forced to go into Rook Hill with her stepmother and stepsisters. When they returned to the house, a horse was tethered in front of it. Lady Isobel looked at it suspiciously but merely herded her daughters upstairs and called for Anya to attend them. Ash dawdled behind, stroking the horse's nose, hoping her stepmother would forget about her. When she went back inside she heard voices coming towards the front hall, and she ducked into the parlour to hide. As they came closer, she realized one of them belonged to the greenwitch, and she sounded upset.

'I think you are making the wrong decision,' said Maire Solanya angrily.

'You have no evidence to support your claims,' Ash's father objected in frustration. 'What you are saying is simply – they are simply tales told to children.'

The greenwitch snorted. 'Very well,' she said coldly.

'If you do not believe what has been true for thousands of years, I cannot change your mind now. But you have to watch out for her – your only daughter. Her mother would have sent her to me in time. Without her mother here to watch over her—'

'She has a stepmother now,' William interrupted.

'That woman knows nothing of this,' Maire Solanya hissed. Ash peered into the hall and saw the greenwitch standing just inside the front door. 'You have lived in Rook Hill long enough to know better,' she said, lowering her voice. 'Letting her sit out there at her mother's grave every night – they will come for her.'

Ash's father did not seem convinced. 'Elinor may have shared your fancies, but I do not,' he said. And then he put his hand on the doorknob in a clear indication that the greenwitch should leave. 'Have a safe journey home.' After he closed the door he sighed, rubbing his eyes. Ash slid back into the parlour before her father turned around, and she tiptoed to the front window. The courtyard was empty; the greenwitch had already left.

Ash wanted to know what Maire Solanya had meant – *who* would come for her? – but she did not dare ask her father. He was restless and aggravated for the rest of the day after the greenwitch's visit. What she had overheard reminded her of the argument he had had with her mother, and she wondered, not for the first time, how many of those tales told to children were true.

Her mother had told her plenty of fairy tales, of course. If they were to be believed, any fairies who still walked this land were most likely to be found deep in the Wood, where no one had travelled for generations. Sometimes at twilight, when Ash was sitting at her mother's grave, she thought she saw things – a silverish shadow, like heat waves in the summer, or the movement of a creature who did not quite set foot upon the ground – but it was only out of the corner of her eye. Whenever she turned to look, there was never anything there. She knew her father would tell her that it was only the fading light playing tricks on her.

So she had been surprised when the book that he brought back for her was a volume of fairy tales. It was bound in dark brown tooled leather, and the frontispiece was a painting of a fairy woman, elegant and pale, wearing a beautiful golden gown. The title of the book was lettered in bold, dark calligraphy: *Tales of Wonder and Grace*. Each story was preceded by a detailed illustration, hand-painted in royal blue and crimson, silver and gilt.

'Thank you,' she said to her father. 'It is beautiful.'

The tales were not all about fairies – some were hunting stories, some were adventures – but many of them were. When her father saw how she was transfixed by the book, he allowed her to skip Ana and Clara's lessons with Lady Isobel. 'She is young,' he said to his new wife, who frowned at this indulgence. 'And she misses her mother. Let her be.'

Ash recognized some of the stories in the book as tales that her mother had told her: *The Golden Ball, The Three Good Advices, The Beast and the Thorn*. But the lengthiest story in the book, *The Farmer and the Hunt*, was unfamiliar to her, and she stared often and long at the illustration that accompanied it. In the picture, a ruddy-faced farmer stood at the edge of a broad field, and riding across it was a ghostly host of hunters outlined in silver paint, their horses' eyes glinting gold. The riders were as pale as the fairy woman on the frontispiece, and their faces were hollow skulls, their mouths gaping open.

In the tale, the farmer, a well-liked man named Thom, vanished on his way home from a village tavern. He was found three days later when one of his neighbours discovered his horse tethered near a wooded copse down by the river. Within the copse, Thom was fast asleep on a bed of dried leaves. Although he was very confused when he awoke, after he had been brought home and fed a good supper, he remembered what had happened. On the night he had disappeared, he waited until the full moon had risen before leaving the tavern, and then he took his customary route home. He was walking past the fallow field west of the Wood when he saw lights dancing in the copse by the river, accompanied by the most beautiful flute music he had ever heard. Because his sweetheart, who had died several years before, had played the flute, Thom was drawn

26

towards the music and wondered who was behind it.

Within the copse he came across a scene so beautiful it made his heart ache. There were sparkling lanterns hanging from the branches, illuminating the clearing where dozens of finely dressed men and women were dancing, their bodies as graceful as blossoms bending in a spring breeze. At first they took no notice of the farmer standing on the edge of their circle, and as his dazzled eyes adjusted to the light, he finally noticed the musicians playing along the sidelines. There was a violinist who played a gilded instrument with finesse, but whose face seemed strangely weary for someone who was making such sweet music. And there was the piper whose flute had called to the farmer; she was a young woman wearing a relatively plain gown in comparison to the dancing ladies. As the farmer gazed at her face, it was as if a glamour slowly fell away from it, and he recognized her as his sweetheart, Grace, who was believed to be dead.

When she looked up and met his eyes, the illusion disappeared, and she put down the flute and came to him. In wonder, he took her hands in his, and her hands were as cold as death. She said to him: 'You must go back, Thom. I am lost to you for ever, but you can still leave.'

As she spoke, the dancing people began to notice him, and one of the women came towards them, her eyes great and blue, and offered him a goblet of wine.

'Will you drink, sir?' she asked sweetly.

He took the goblet without thinking, and the girl departed, but just as he was about to take a sip Grace said urgently, 'You must not drink of that wine. If you do you will be trapped for ever in this world, never to see your family again.'

Her words made him hesitate, but he said, 'I had thought you were lost to me; where is this place I have come to?'

'You have stepped into fairy land,' she answered. 'Three years ago, I was walking home one night when I encountered the Fairy Hunt, and they offered to take me the rest of the way. I should not have believed them. As soon as I mounted one of their horses, they took me to Taninli, their home, where they gave me food and drink. I was so hungry and thirsty that I gave in, but now I must serve them for eternity, for no humans are allowed to taste their delicacies.'

'I will join you,' he said, 'for I love you and would be with you for eternity.'

But she shook her head, and her eyes were dark with pain. 'I am but a shadow of myself and can never love you as a human could,' she said. 'The fairies have taken my heart away from me.'

He could see that she told the truth, for no blood warmed her skin, and there was no pulse beating in her throat. Yet a part of him still wished to be with her regardless of what form she had taken, and when she saw this in his heart, she led him out of the copse, fearing for his safety, and took the goblet away from his hand. 'You must forget about me from now on, and if you see the Fairy Hunt riding, never approach them,' she warned him. And then she touched his cheek and he fell down in an enchanted sleep and did not awaken until his neighbour discovered him.

But as is the way with these encounters, Thom could not forget what he had seen, and every night he yearned for Grace, his heart aching anew. At last he took to wandering near the wooded copse by the river, hoping to hear Grace's flute. One night at twilight, Thom saw a dozen ghostly riders coming towards him, and soon he recognized them as the Fairy Hunt. But he ignored Grace's words of warning and gladly went to meet them. After that night he was never seen again, and no one knows if he succeeded in finding his way back to Grace. But a month later, the same neighbour who had awakened Thom from his enchanted sleep came across the farmer again, except this time he would not awaken, for he was dead.

The *Tales of Wonder and Grace* only sparked more questions in Ash. At night when she sat beside her mother's grave, wondering if this would be the night that someone – something – came to take her away, as Maire Solanya had warned, she watched the darkness gathering in the nearby trees with equal parts dread and anticipation. What lay beyond those trees? Would she ever dare to do what Thom had done? If the stories were true, as Maire Solanya had seemed to imply, then there might be a way to see her mother again.

There were some common threads among the fairy tales she had read. Fairies were drawn to in-between times like Midsummer's Eve, when the full weight of summer begins to tip towards the shorter days of autumn; or Souls Night, when the spirits of the newly departed walk the land. But fairies were never seen in common daylight, and they preferred the light of the full moon for their hunts and celebrations. So on the night of the next full moon, Ash rose from her bed at midnight, trembling with excitement. She pulled on her woollen cloak and tiptoed halfway down the upstairs corridor before her stepsister's door cracked open. She heard Ana's voice whispering, 'Where are you going?' Ash froze, turning to look at her stepsister. Ana was peering out at her curiously, holding a lit candle stub beneath her face.

'It's none of your business,' Ash whispered. 'Go back to bed.'

Ana's eyes narrowed and she stepped out into the corridor, pulling her door shut behind her. She observed, 'You are dressed to go outside. Where do you think you're going?'

'I can go wherever I want,' Ash said curtly.

She turned her back on her stepsister and began

to walk towards the stairs, but stopped when Ana said, 'I'll tell. I'll wake up your father and tell him you're going out.'

Anger rose inside her – she would *not* let this girl stop her – and she glared at Ana. 'Do whatever you like,' Ash said dismissively. She did not wait for Ana's reaction but went down the stairs quickly, her heart racing with fear and exhilaration.

In the pantry, she lit the covered lantern before going to the back door. She put her hand on the doorknob and looked behind her. In the glow of the lantern the kitchen was comforting and ordinary. Ana had not followed her. Taking a deep breath, she turned the doorknob and plunged out into the night.

As she went down toward the Wood, the full moon hung like a giant, pale eye above her, unwavering in its gaze. At the foot of the hill, she paused and looked up at the house, and the windows were dark, reflecting only the heavy moon. The lantern threw her shadow up the hill, a black ghost attached to her feet, and she shivered as the wind came rattling through the pine branches. Steeling herself, she turned towards the Wood and her mother's grave, and just beyond it was the track she and her mother had sometimes taken to gather mushrooms or wild plants. They had never gone far enough to lose sight of the house, and Ash did not know how far the path went, but tonight she meant to find out.

Entering the Wood was like entering a vast cavern:

The sound of her footsteps was magnified by the branches arching above. Her lantern cast only a tiny glow in the immense black, for now she could no longer see the moon. As she went deeper into the trees, she heard the call of a night owl, and an animal bounded through the undergrowth – a rabbit? – In the distance, the howl of a wolf raised the hairs on the back of her neck. She thought she could see eyes glowing on the trail ahead of her, but a moment later they had slid to the right, and she could not follow them as well as keep her eyes on the path. Her hands trembled and made the lantern bob, casting wild shadows on the ground, but she pressed on and tried to ignore the frightened voice in her head that told her to go back. Moving made her feel better: at least she could run.

She came to a tangle of fallen branches that blocked her way, and in order to continue she had to leave the path to pick her away around them. The ground was uneven, with roots protruding from the forest floor, and when she reached out to steady herself on a nearby tree trunk she felt something move beneath her fingers. She gasped in fright and hastened forward, clinging to the lantern, suddenly afraid she would drop it and be left in the pitch-black night.

She did not know how long she had been walking before she realized she had lost her way back to the path. She was standing among tall trunks of blue pine, their bark mottled grey and black in the lantern light, and this time when she turned to look around herself at the waiting dark, she was sure that she saw something glittering back at her: eyes, yellow and blinking. She heard her own breath, quick and frantic, like a hunted creature. And then the whispering began. It came on the wind, sweeping toward her in scratchy bursts, and then was borne away again before she could discern any words. She held out the lantern like a weapon, calling out, 'Who is there?'

There was the sound of laughter – thin, distant, like bells. Was this the sign she had been seeking? She turned towards the sound and stumbled forward, tripping over the undergrowth. As the laughter came more frequently, the whispering began to separate out into sentences spoken in a language she did not understand. It could only be the fairies, she thought, for who else would be deep in the Wood at midnight? The thought raised a cold sweat on her skin, for if they were real, then all the consequences in those tales must be real, too. But that was the last clear thought she had, because then she saw the lights in the distance. They did not waver; they were beacons in the night. She started to walk towards them, but they always seemed just out of reach. She began to feel a deep longing in the pit of her stomach: When would she get there? She feared she would wander in the dark Wood for ever, until she was only a skeleton powered by sheer will.

That was when the drumbeat of horses' hooves came

towards her, the ground rumbling with the force of their passage. She stood transfixed, and the wind rose, buffeting her in cold gusts. It became more difficult to see, as if there were a fog rising, and just when the horses seemed to be nearly upon her, her lantern went out, leaving her momentarily blind. But soon afterwards the fog began to glow with an otherworldly light, and she shivered in its damp chill. When she saw the first horse, she felt her heart leap up into her throat. This moment would be fixed in her memory for ever: the moment she saw with her own eyes the creatures she had heard about all her life. They were grand and beautiful and frightening – the horses' heads shining white, their eyes burning like a blacksmith's forge. The riders, too, were like nothing she had ever seen before: ethereal men and women with pale visages, their cheekbones so sharply sculpted that she could see their skulls through translucent skin. They surrounded her and looked at her with steely blue eyes, each gaze an arrow staking her to that spot, and she could not close her eyes though the sight of them made her eyes burn as if she were looking at the sun.

They seemed to speak to each other, but she could not see their mouths moving, and she could only hear the strange, uneven whispering she had heard before. Suddenly the riders moved in unison, circling her, and she felt like she was being spun like a limp doll held by a wilful child. When the motion stopped, the riders were streaming away from her in an elegant spiral, leaving her alone with one man who looked down at her from his tall white horse. He was more handsome than any man she had ever seen, but like the other riders, he was pale as a ghost. When he spoke, she was stunned that she could understand him, and he said, 'You must go back.'

She opened her mouth to say, 'I came to find you.' It felt as though she hadn't spoken in years.

He looked deeply angry, and she covered beneath his glare. He said: 'Then you are a fool.'

She sank to her knees and begged, 'Please – listen to me—'

He extended his arm, pointing back the way she had come. 'Go now – the way is clear to you. And do not return.' She felt herself scramble to her feet as if he had picked her up, and behind her the path was clear through the Wood. At the end of it, in the far distance, a light in the kitchen window gleamed. She felt the force of the air behind her, propelling her to turn around, and her legs took her at breakneck speed down the path. It was wide open, free of pebbles or fallen branches or even the thick padding of last year's leaves. She could not slow down, and she could not look back, either. The ground was hard and cold beneath her feet, and when she burst through the border of the Wood and came upon the hawthorn tree, it was as if she had been slapped forward by the wind and forbidden to return.

The lantern was dead in her hand, and the Wood was a stone wall behind her.

Anya was standing at the top of the hill, calling her name, and when she saw Ash coming up the hill she ran down to meet her. 'Where have you been?' she cried. 'Ana said you ran away – are you all right?' She bent toward Ash and pulled her into an embrace. 'Aisling,' she said in a ragged voice, 'your father – he is not well.'

'What do you mean?' Ash demanded, pushing her away. 'What do you mean he's not well?'

'The greenwitch is here,' Anya said. 'Maire Solanya is here. She has given him a draught to calm him, but he shouts in his fever.'

Ash ran into the house and upstairs, down the hallway lit with flaming sconces and into her father's room, where he lay in bed tossing and turning, the greenwitch chanting something unfamiliar yet unmistakably old. Lady Isobel sat in the window seat, turned away from them. Maire Solanya saw Ash and halted her chanting, coming towards her. 'This is a sickroom, Ash,' she said. 'You must stay away.' And she pushed Ash out of the room and closed the door.

Standing in the hallway, Ash could hear her father shouting. It sounded like he was calling for her mother.

4

The fever lasted for two days. But a week after it broke, Ash's father had still not recovered, and Maire Solanya returned to speak with Lady Isobel. Hovering outside her father's room, Ash heard their voices rise with emotion.

'Nothing you have done has worked,' Lady Isobel said bitterly. 'Why should I follow this new course of treatment? He has not improved.'

'You are not understanding what has afflicted him,' Maire Solanya said. 'He is only now coming out of the worst of it. He must continue to drink this.'

'It has only made him feel worse,' Lady Isobel said. 'I won't allow it.'

'With all due respect, madam, he is too ill to decide for himself, and you do not understand what I am trying to do. You must let me make the decisions in this matter.'

'I understand that your old-fashioned ways are not working,' Lady Isobel said harshly, clearly frustrated. 'I think it is best that I send for a physician.'

'But they will bleed him,' Maire Solanya objected. 'That will only make him weaker.'

'You do not understand medicine,' Lady Isobel said derisively. 'It will clear out the bad blood.'

'You will kill him if you do that,' the greenwitch said, her tone low and hard. 'Is that what you wish to do?'

Suddenly the footsteps came towards the door, which was wrenched open. Lady Isobel stood on the other side, her hand on the doorknob, visibly shaking. 'Get out of my house,' she snapped at Maire Solanya. 'Get out!'

Ash had not moved quickly enough; she stood in the corridor, gaping at the two women. Maire Solanya did not say another word, but only swept through the doorway. When she passed Ash, frozen in the hallway, she briefly touched her shoulder as if to reassure her. But then Lady Isobel saw Ash and demanded, 'What are you doing there? Have you been eavesdropping? Go to your room!'

'I want to see my father,' Ash said stubbornly.

Her stepmother's face darkened with anger and she pointed down the hall towards Ash's chamber. 'Go to your room. Now. Your father will send for you when he wishes to see you.' But she did not even wait to see if Ash had obeyed; instead she went back inside, closed the door, and, a moment later, slid the bolt in place.

Ash had not slept well since her walk in the Wood. After Maire Solanya had shut her out of her father's room, she had lain sleepless in her bed until the sun rose. Every night since then, she was haunted by the fear that she had somehow made things worse by seeking out the Fairy Hunt. When she closed her eyes she could see the eerie grace of the riders as if they were circling her bed at night.

When she finally fell asleep, she slept deeply, and waking up was like dragging herself through mud. Sometimes she awoke gasping for air as if she had been in the midst of a nightmare, but she could not remember what she had dreamed. One morning she was pulled out of her uneasy, thick sleep by a steady pounding that sharpened into a knocking at her bedroom door. She blinked her eyes open, her gaze unfocussed, and saw her stepsister, Ana, in the doorway. The morning light coming through the window was gray and watery, giving her skin an unhealthy pallor. She said, 'Mother says we must hurry and pack up our things. Your father is not well and he must see a physician in the Royal City.'

Ash was confused. 'What – what do you mean?'

'We're going home,' Ana said. 'Finally.'

They packed the trunks that morning, first dragging them up from the cellar and then – loudly – back downstairs again. Lady Isobel said they would return in the spring, so Ash packed her two books of fairy tales and all her winter dresses. Anya was not going. Lady Isobel had her own manor house near the City and her own housekeeper there. Instead, Anya would stay behind to close up the house for the winter, and then she would go back to Rook Hill and stay with her daughter. All that day, Ash felt an underlying sense of surprise: She had never imagined the possibility that she might leave Rook Hill. And she was not ready to go.

By noon the carriage had arrived, and the driver helped Anya load their trunks onto the rack. After a cold, hurried lunch eaten in silence, Ash stood on the front stoop, waiting, and felt like her entire world was being erased. Anya came out and put her arms around her and said, 'Lady Isobel will take good care of you.'

She hugged Anya close, with tears pricking her eyes. 'I don't want to go,' she whispered.

'Hush,' Anya said, smoothing her hand over Ash's hair. 'It's the best for your father.' She put her hands on Ash's shoulders and looked down at her. 'You be a good girl, Ash.' She kissed her on her forehead.

Her father came outside, supported by Lady Isobel and the driver. Ash had not seen him in nearly two weeks, and he looked, in that noon light, like an old man; she was shocked by the change in him.

They drove for a week, pausing only to rest the horses. Ash's father slept for most of the journey, and when he awoke he was often disoriented. On the first day they left the Northern Mountains behind, heading south toward the King's Highway. On the second day the land widened until all that Ash could see from one horizon to another was spreading golden fields ready for harvest. Then the broad fields gave way to softly rolling hills covered with orchards, and through the carriage windows Ash watched the fruit being plucked from the trees, red and round.

They arrived at Quinn House in the village of West Riding well after dark, and as soon as the carriage pulled to a halt at the end of the long drive, Lady Isobel leapt out, calling for assistance. A man came to help her bring Ash's father inside, and Clara and Ana ran after them, excited to be home. A woman wearing an apron came towards the carriage holding a lantern and shone it at her, saying gruffly, 'You must be the new girl. Come inside.' Ash climbed out of the carriage in a daze; she saw a large stone building before her, the front door yawning open. The woman took Ash upstairs, leading her down a dim corridor to a dark room. 'This is your room,' she said, lighting a candle for her. 'You may as well go to bed; it's late.' She shut the door behind her.

The room was plainly furnished with simple wooden furniture; in addition to the small bed there was a wardrobe beside the door, and beneath the casement window was a cushioned bench. She lay down on the bed, pulling her travelling cloak over herself. The blanket beneath her was rough and thin; the bed was hard and creaked when she moved. Conscious of the long days they had traveled, she felt very far from Rook Hill. The distance awoke a longing in her like a cord pulled suddenly taut: She wanted so much to go back.

She leaned over and blew out the candle, but sleep did not come quickly enough.

The first thing she saw when she woke up was her trunk: It had been delivered while she was asleep, and it sat locked and still beside the wardrobe. She got out of bed and went to the window, pushing open the dark brown draperies. To her surprise, outside the window she saw a forest – the southern end of the Wood. There was no sloping hillside as there had been in Rook Hill; here the land was flat, and between the house and the trees was a meadow, the grasses golden and knee-high. She saw a kitchen garden below, planted in neat squares marked off in red brick; a profusion of herbs staked out territory directly below her window. Ash twisted the window lock and pushed open the diamond-paned glass, leaning out into the morning. It was cool outside, and the scent of the air was new to her – meadow grass mingled with herbs from the garden. She took a deep breath and hoped that her father would regain his health here.

The physicians, however, were not as hopeful. They were already in the house that morning; Ash could hear the murmur of their voices from down the hall when she came out of her room. They drew her father's blood and gave him a noxious-smelling tea to drink, and she could hear him coughing. She heard the physicians say that the journey must have tired him out, but her father did not regain his strength. They let her in to see him, and he did not recognize her; his eyes were milky and distant.

He died almost two weeks later. Ash woke up that morning with her heart pounding, and she knew that something was wrong because the house was full of noise. She threw back the covers and jumped out of bed, running down the hallway towards her father's room. A black-robed physician with a long, moody face was opening his door, and when he saw her approaching he said, 'This is not the place for you.'

'What's going on?' she asked.

'Your father does not need you now,' the physician said, trying to block her way. But Ash slipped around him and pushed through the doorway. Her father's body was convulsing out of control, and red spittle dotted his cheeks and the snow-white sheets that were pulled up to his chin. He was being held down by two physicians, one on either side of him, and Lady Isobel stood as far from him as possible, her hands covering her mouth.

Ash ran toward the bed as the third physician tried to stop her again, and she clutched at her father's twitching right hand. 'Father,' she said in a frightened voice. 'Father, what is wrong?' His cheeks were pale and sunken, and bandages covered his wrists. 'What have you done to him?' she demanded, recalling Maire Solanya's distrust of the physicians' methods.

'He is ill,' one of them said. 'You must leave.'

Then there were two pairs of hands holding her shoulders back, and though she screamed for them to let her go to her father, they dragged her from the room and slammed the door in her face. She pounded at the door when she heard the lock click shut, crying, 'Let me in!' But they did not answer.

She stood there for what seemed like hours, tears slowly leaking from her eyes, her bare feet growing colder minute by minute. And then there was a great noise, followed by silence, and the sound of Lady Isobel sobbing.

Two men from the village church came to take her father's body away later that morning. Lady Isobel came down from her bedroom dressed in black, a veil covering her face, and announced that the funeral would take place the next day in the church at noon. Ash's father would be buried in the cemetery, and Lady Isobel told her there was no need for an overnight vigil. 'You must leave your superstitions behind now,' her stepmother said sternly.

At the funeral, Ash wore the stiff black dress that Lady Isobel gave her; the collar felt like hands around her throat. She sat still, looking down at the floorboards, too stunned to cry. Although there was a service led by the village philosopher, Ash did not hear a word of it. She felt smothered by the church walls, and as soon as she could escape outside she did, taking deep breaths of the muggy air.

Behind the church, a rectangular pit in the ground gaped open, awaiting her father's body. His gravestone was not ready yet; until it was carved, his grave would be marked by the banner that flew now, waist high, a splash of red against the slate-coloured sky. When the mourners began to throw handfuls of earth onto the body, Ash had to look away.

When it was over, they climbed back into the carriage and returned to Quinn House. The glowering sky hinted of rain, and it had grown colder. Ash went upstairs to her bedroom; the house smelled of the bitter medicines the physicians had brewed. In her room, she opened the window and curled up on the seat beneath it, waiting for the first drops of rain to fall. It smelled like moss and oak and the damp dark spaces of the Wood beyond the meadow. She looked out at the wide expanse of golden grass being lashed by the rising wind, and wondered whether Anya had closed all the windows in their house in Rook Hill.

She thought: *Now, I am all alone.*

5

Everything changed after her father died. Ash had known every inch of her home in Rook Hill; Quinn House was strange and large and cold. In Rook Hill, everyone knew and cherished her mother and father; here, she was pitied by others: *Poor girl. Orphan.* Though Lady Isobel had never treated her with much fondness, now that Ash's father was gone, she no longer tried to hide her disapproval. And West Riding itself was a world away from Rook Hill, which was small and sleepy and content to be nothing more than that. West Riding, scarcely five miles from the Royal City, was known far and wide as the staging ground for the Royal Hunt – and hunting season had already begun.

Rook Hill had its own hunt and its own huntress, of course, for hunts had always been led by women. But Ash had never seen a hunting party as grand as the Royal Hunt. Not a day went by that fall without the sounds of hunting horns in the distance. When she saw the hunters in the village, Ash was transfixed by the sight of them. The women, especially, with their casual camaraderie and easy grace, seemed like entirely different creatures than her stepmother and stepsisters.

Autumn turned into winter, and Lady Isobel had the rest of their things sent down from Rook Hill. The day the trunks arrived was a harsh reminder to Ash of how much her life had changed since the summer. When she opened her trunk, it smelled of the house at Rook Hill, and it all came back: the way her father smiled at her on her birthday. The sound of her mother's laughter. The time she and her parents had walked into Rook Hill on an autumn day, the leaves as gold as coins, the air crisp and dry. When the memories came, Ash felt her heart constrict as if she were being bound by ropes so tight she would lose all breath. It hurt in a way she had never felt before, and she did not know how to make it stop.

As Yule approached, with all of its attendant memories – the smell of pastries in the oven, the spicy tang of pine boughs in the house – she thought the pain might never cease. Yule week in Rook Hill was celebrated with nightly gatherings at different houses throughout the village, where friends and family shared stories about the years past. The week culminated in a masque, where the villagers dressed in fantastical costumes as kings and queens and witches and fairies, going from door to door to bring each family to the bonfire in the village green. Ash had loved the roar of the fire – it sounded like a wild beast, crackling and growling and hot as summer.

She remembered her mother, dressed in a paper crown and red velvet cloak, blowing kisses across the flames to her father, dressed as a joker with gold and silver baubles hanging from his cap.

This winter, Yule would be a much more subdued affair. 'Out of respect for my husband's untimely passing,' Lady Isobel declared. She would refrain from wearing a costume, though she had ordered matching shepherdess dresses for Ana and Clara. 'You must wear your black dress,' Lady Isobel told Ash one night at supper. 'It is not right for you to celebrate this year.'

All week Beatrice and the chambermaid, Sara, had been at work in the kitchen, preparing pastries and sweetmeats for Lady Isobel's feast on Yule night. Ash and Ana and Clara waited in the parlour, watching as the musicians set up in the front hall. Shortly before the first guests arrived, Lady Isobel came downstairs dressed in a gown of black velvet and lace, with a headdress made of black feathers rising from her auburn hair. Even Ash had to admit that she was an imposing figure, and when she gathered Ana and Clara to her to kiss their beribboned heads, Ash felt like a sparrow among peacocks.

That night the house was full of light and noise, with people dressed as soldiers and queens and dancers and chieftains. Ash watched them laughing and dancing from her corner in the front hall, and no one noticed her. Halfway through the evening there was a pounding on the front door, and when Lady Isobel opened it there seemed to be a gang of thieves on the doorstep – half a dozen men dressed in worn leather with caps pulled low over their heads, and hands that seemed to be stained with blood. Even Lady Isobel recoiled at the unexpected ferocity of these visitors, until the men were pushed aside and a woman dressed in hunting gear threw back her green hooded cloak to reveal a smiling face. 'Don't mind my men,' she said, bowing to Lady Isobel, her dark blond hair falling over her shoulder in a thick braid. 'We come bearing new meat – in return, of course, for a drink or two.' The men behind her cheered loudly and thrust forward into the room, one of them carrying the head of a stag, its dead eyes glassy, the tongue hanging out of its slightly open mouth.

Visibly shaken, Lady Isobel called for Beatrice to attend them, and Ash wondered if it was customary in West Riding for the hunt to come in like that, all bloody and fresh from the kill. But Beatrice came forward without a word and led two of the men and their haunch of venison into the kitchen. The man with the stag's head began to go into the parlour, but the huntress caught his arm and said something to him in a curt, low tone of voice, and he looked sheepish and took the head outside. The huntress saw Ash then, standing with her back to the wall. She must have had a stricken expression on her face because the huntress smiled at her and said, 'I'm sorry if my boys frightened you.

They mean no harm; they've just been in the Wood for too long.'

'I'm not frightened,' Ash said, although she had been, just a little. 'Did you hunt all day?'

'Yes,' the huntress said, pulling off her cloak and beginning to yank off her thick leather gloves. 'But it's all right if you were afraid,' she said with a sideways look at Ash. 'It's smart to be afraid of things that smell of death.' She came closer to the girl and bent toward her, putting a firm hand on Ash's shoulder. 'Just don't be afraid to look them in the eye,' she said with a grin, and then ruffled Ash's hair before moving on into the dining room. No one else had paid the slightest attention to her all night, and Ash felt as though the huntress had suddenly called her into being. She slid out from her corner and went after her, watching as the huntress took a seat at the long table with one of her men and a masked reveller dressed as a queen. When they saw Ash standing hesitantly nearby, the man asked, 'Whose child is that?'

The huntress looked over at her. 'Come and sit with us,' she said.

The woman dressed as a queen smiled at her and asked, 'Are you hungry?'

Ash shook her head but came and sat next to the huntress as Sara poured wine into their goblets. 'Where is your costume tonight?' the huntress asked. All around them the guests were dressed as princesses or lords, their masks glittering with garnets and plumed with feathers.

'I do not have one,' Ash answered.

'Poor thing,' said the masked queen. 'She needs cheering up.'

'You could tell her a story,' the man prompted, looking at the huntress.

The masked queen said, 'Yes, a story – a hunting story!'

The huntress grinned and asked Ash, 'Is that what you'd like?'

Ash coloured, but said, 'Yes, I would.'

'Very well, then,' said the huntress. 'I will tell you the story of Eilis and the Changeling. Do you know that tale?'

Ash shook her head.

'Eilis was one of our earliest huntresses; King Roland called her to service when she was only eighteen, and many people questioned whether she was ready to lead the Royal Hunt,' the huntress explained. 'The same year that Eilis was chosen, the Queen gave birth to her first child, a girl. But on the morning after the princess was born, the Queen went to suckle her child, and she would not eat. Days passed and the princess continued to refuse her mother's milk, and yet she did not weaken. Instead, her skin turned a curious golden color, and she seemed to grow at an astonishing speed. The greenwitches were consulted, and they concluded that the princess had been stolen and replaced with a fairy changeling.'

'Fairies and greenwitches,' said the masked queen. 'This is a fairy tale, not a hunting story.'

The huntress covered the woman's hand with her own and said, 'Patience. There will be hunters.' She looked back at Ash and continued: 'The King and Queen tried everything they could to trick the changeling into revealing its true identity, for that was the only way to bring the real princess back. But nothing worked, and as the months passed they began to fear they would never see their daughter again. Now, some greenwitches remembered that there might be one other way to bring the young princess back, but it would require someone to journey to Taninli and beg the Fairy Queen to return the child. When Eilis heard this, she knew that she must be the one to go, for this was how she could earn the people's trust. She told the King and Queen of her intention, and though they were apprehensive, they longed for their daughter's return and agreed to Eilis's plan.'

'What happened to the changeling?' Ash asked curiously.

The huntress paused. 'I don't know,' she answered. 'I suppose the changeling remained in the princess's place. At any rate, Eilis entered the Wood on the day after Souls Night, and though many doubted she would ever return, on the morning of Yule she was seen riding through the gates of the Royal City with a babe in her arms. The King and Queen were shocked when she came before them, for she had aged nearly a decade, though she had only been absent two months. She told them that when she entered the Wood she had ridden for a fortnight seeking out the centre of the great forest, where she discovered a small trail paved with white stones. It eventually became a broad avenue lined with trees she had never seen before and ended in a set of huge crystal gates – she knew she had arrived at Taninli.'

'When she told the fairy guard that she sought an audience with the Fairy Queen, she was taken to a massive palace built of crystal. In the Queen's audience chamber, Eilis knelt down and asked for the return of the princess. The Queen told Eilis that her wish would be granted only if she completed three tasks successfully: She must retrieve a gryphon's egg from its nest; she must bring the Fairy Queen a living unicorn; and she must hunt the great white stag and bring back its head. If she succeeded, the princess would be returned.'

'So Eilis set out to fulfill those tasks, and none of them was easy. But she had an advantage that the Fairy Queen did not anticipate: She was young and determined, and she did not know that she could fail. Though it took many months for her to find a gryphon – for they were few and far between even in Eilis's time – she did find one at last, and she artfully stole the gold-plated egg from beneath the sleeping beast itself. Though it took many months, she did find a unicorn and lured it, with honey and sweet songs, back to the Fairy Queen. And though it took many months, she tracked down a white stag whose rack was as wide as the avenue in Taninli, and she slew him with her small human-made sword. In the end, the Fairy Queen had to honour her words, and she delivered the young princess, no worse for wear, into Eilis's arms.'

'The princess was still a baby?' Ash interrupted. 'Even though so much time had passed?'

'Yes,' said the huntress. 'Time passes differently, it is said, among the fairies. And there was always the suspicion, afterward, that the princess had become something more than human during her time with the Fairy Queen. When Eilis returned to the Royal City with the princess, there was a grand celebration and Eilis went back to her duty as the King's Huntress. From that time onward, fewer changelings were found in the country, for the fairies don't like to lose what they have stolen.' The huntress took a drink from her goblet when she finished her tale, and the two revellers seated with her clapped their hands.

'A wonderful story,' said the woman in delight.

'Did you like it?' the man asked Ash.

'Yes,' Ash said, and it gave her an idea. She hesitated for a moment and then asked the huntress, 'Have *you* seen a fairy?' In the weeks since her father had died, Ash's memory of her midnight encounter with the Fairy Hunt had seemed more like a dream than reality.

Sometimes she tried to remember what that man had looked like – the one who had spoken to her – but the shape of his face kept sliding away from her mind's eye. Now, looking at the huntress, she thought that if anyone could confirm what she had seen, it would be her.

The huntress seemed surprised by her question. 'I am afraid I have not,' she said.

Ash was disappointed, and her face fell. The masked queen said quickly, 'But you've said, haven't you, that sometimes you see things in the Wood?'

The huntress smiled. 'I cannot say if those things were fairies.'

'But they were unusual?' the woman teased.

'Indeed, they were unusual,' the huntress affirmed.

'How?' Ash asked.

The huntress put down her goblet and looked at Ash intently. 'Sometimes,' she said, 'at twilight, or in the shade, the light plays tricks. Once I saw something that looked like a woman with wings.'

'A wood sprite,' exclaimed the woman.

'Perhaps,' the huntress said. Another hunter came into the dining room then and bent down to whisper in her ear, and the huntress stood up. 'I am afraid the time for stories is at an end,' she said to Ash, and her companions also rose to leave. 'Good night,' she said, and briefly bowed her head to Ash.

'Goodnight,' Ash answered, feeling let down. Was that

all she had seen? She watched them go, their green-and-brown hunting gear the only solemn colours among the costumed guests, and then went back upstairs. She would rather be alone in her room than alone in the midst of a celebration she was not a part of.

It was a week later that the letters came: two of them, thick and bound with black ribbon, stamped with an ornate red seal. Ash saw them lying on the hall table before Lady Isobel took them into the parlour to read on her own. Ash was at her lessons with Ana and Clara in the library when Beatrice opened the door and said, 'Ash, Lady Isobel would like to see you right now.' Ash glanced at her stepsisters, but they seemed as surprised as she was.

In the parlour, a fire was burning in the hearth, but the room was still chilly. A candleabra was lit at the writing desk by the window where her stepmother sat. The letters were open before her, and when Ash came closer and looked at the seal again, she thought they looked familiar.

'Do you recognize something?' Lady Isobel inquired as Ash sat down in a stiff-backed chair next to the desk.

'They look like my father's seals,' Ash replied.

'This one is.' Lady Isobel picked up a letter and held it up to the light. 'It is from your father's steward in Seatown.' She picked up the second letter and said, 'This one is from the King's treasurer in the City.'

Her face wore a look of grim decision. 'Do you know what this means?'

Ash shook her head.

'Your father's business was not doing well when he died,' Lady Isobel said bitterly, 'and he spent my inheritance on it. I did not know this until now. This letter says that your father has debts that I must pay for him now that he has died.' Her voice took on a steely quality as she said, 'I do not have the money to pay for your father's mistakes. My first husband left me with only this property to support me; that is why I married your father, because I thought he was a good man who would provide for me and my daughters. But he was a liar.'

Ash objected, 'He was not. You —'

'Be quiet,' her stepmother said. 'I am telling you these things because you need to know what sort of family you come from. You are not my daughter; you are your father's daughter, and you are going to pay his debts.'

'What — what do you mean?' Ash asked in a thin voice.

'Because of these taxes, I must sell your father's house in Rook Hill,' her stepmother said. 'It is of no use to me. That will solve some of these problems, but not all of them. I could send you out to service in the City, but I can make better use of you here. Therefore you will start by helping Beatrice in the kitchen every morning. In the afternoon you will review Ana and Clara's lessons on your own, and then you will assist Beatrice in preparing and serving supper.' Lady Isobel paused, and then looked directly at Ash before saying, 'If your father had known how to manage his finances better, you would not be put in the position of paying for his mistakes. As it is, I will expect you to work off his debts without complaint, because you are his daughter and it is your responsibility. Do not shirk your duties.'

Ash was silent. She felt numb.

Lady Isobel folded the letters and put them in the desk drawer. 'Now go and find Beatrice. I've already told her about this; she'll need you to help her tonight because Sara won't be coming here again. I can't afford to pay Sara when you can do the work instead.'

Ash stood up and left the cold parlour, and went slowly to the kitchen. Beatrice was pulling the stew pot off the stove, and when she saw Ash hovering in the doorway she said, 'Come over here, girl, and give me a hand. Lady Isobel told me you're to work with me now.'

Ash went toward the broad wooden table where Beatrice had set the pot down.

'Get the plates and bowls from the cupboard,' Beatrice ordered. 'Don't just stand there.'

Ash went to the cupboard and took out the plates she was accustomed to eating on. The stew smelled like thyme and roast mutton that night, and when Beatrice lifted the lid, the fragrant steam wafted up in a hot cloud. Beatrice dished out the stew into three bowls and began to slice the bread. 'Take that out to the dining room and light the candles,' Beatrice said, gesturing to the bowls.

The dining room was dark and Ash lit the candles with shaking hands. As the room came into light, it was as if the world had shifted: three place settings, three chairs, three plates. There had never really been a place for her, after all. She went to tell Ana and Clara to come for supper.

6

As the winter passed, Ash learned the feel of firewood in the morning, the cold bark digging into her fingers as she carried the rough logs upstairs, depositing them one by one into each bedroom. She learned how to set the tinder in place so that the wood caught fire as quickly as possible; she learned how to breathe gently on the first sparks to coax them into flame. Her fingers became calloused from scrubbing the hall floor, and she learned how to carry the heavy bucket of soapy water up the stairs without spilling a drop. When she flung the dirty water out the kitchen door, she watched the brown liquid soak into the ground where it left a stain on what remained of the snow. And she came to know the corners of the drafty stone house well. On the first floor landing there was a chip in the plaster where a dark hole opened up in the wall just above the floor, and sometimes she would lie flat on her belly and peer into the darkness. In the parlor, the window seat lifted up to reveal a locked chest carved with vines and roses; the keyhole was wedged shut with a wad of tissue, and she could never quite pry it out.

When she had first begun to work, she had been clumsy and slow. She knocked her knees against the bucket, bruising them. She cut her hands on the firewood and nearly singed off her eyelashes while fanning the morning flames. Her stepmother berated her for her mistakes, and initially Ash would reply sharply, but each time she felt the sting of her stepmother's ringed hand on her cheek, she sank further into silence. Once, as Beatrice was sponging off a cut on the corner of Ash's mouth that had been delivered by her stepmother's hand, she said gruffly, 'You're making things harder on yourself. It does no good to anger her.' Ash looked at the housekeeper, whose mouth was set in a frown. Sometimes Ash felt as though her own heart were frozen. She did not dare to let herself feel a thing except anger, because that warmed her. But in that moment she saw the hint of tenderness on the older woman's face, and the grief inside her reared up again, coming out of her in a broken sob.

Beatrice looked startled, and Ash covered her face with her hands, pressing the emotion back down. 'It hurts, does it?' Beatrice said, not unkindly. 'It'll heal up sooner than you think.'

That winter seemed to stretch on interminably, but spring finally crept back to West Riding to suffuse the meadow in a glow of pale green. Ash's thirteenth birthday was shortly after the Spring Festival, when flower peddlers flooded the market square with buckets of daffodils and crocuses. In Rook Hill, her mother would have woken her up with gifts wrapped in silk, but this year Ash woke up alone just as dawn broke and dressed quickly in the dim light of her bedroom. She went outside to the pump and paused in the kitchen garden, smelling the spring air: the sharp tang of the herb garden, the slight sweetness of new meadow grass, the trace of damp that lingered from the morning dew. She had dreamed the night before that she was walking down the hard-packed dirt path that led from the Wood to the hawthorn tree where her mother was buried. She could see the headstone, but though she kept walking, she could never reach the end of the path.

She had dreamed that same dream many times over the course of the winter, but in recent days, it had become more insistent. Now she stood in the garden looking out across the meadow at the budding trees of the King's Forest, and she felt something inside of her turning toward those trees. Perhaps, she thought, she could just leave.

The idea sent a jolt through her, and she glanced back at the house as if someone might have overheard her thoughts. But all she saw was the kitchen door hanging partway open. Taking a deep breath, Ash picked up the wooden bucket and went to the pump, where she lifted the cold iron handle, creaking, to release a flood of icy water. Her hands trembled.

The opportunity came a week after her birthday. Lady Isobel had taken her daughters to luncheon with the village philosopher, and Beatrice had gone into the City on an errand. Ash stood at the front door and watched the carriage roll away with her stepmother and stepsisters inside, and then she shut the door after them. The house was silent. She took her cloak and went out the kitchen door and did not look back.

It was a pleasant, warm day, and the sun was nearly overhead. The herbs brushed against her skirt as she went down the path and out the low iron gate to the meadow. She thought that if she walked along the border of the Wood she would eventually come to another village where she could hire a carriage with the promise of payment upon arrival in Rook Hill. But when she reached the treeline she felt a compulsion to continue into the forest instead of turning west. The sound of birds was clear in the air; the sun dappled the ground in patches of yellow and light green; the new leaves whispered gently when the breeze rustled through. The trail was carpeted in a slightly damp layer of fallen leaves from last autumn, and the ground was spongy beneath her feet. As she walked into the rich smell of sunlight and growing things, a path opened wide before her like an old carriage road just rediscovered.

Her original plan, tentative though it was, had been forgotten. Her feet moved as if of their own will, and she felt a dim sense of surprise that she was so sure of her destination: straight forward along the path, where the distance lay shadowed in green and yellow and brown, magnetic in its mystery. All around her she felt the Wood breathing, her senses alive. It was as if she could see the leaves unfurling gracefully from their jewel-like buds, the young beetles creeping purposefully forward on the earth. She did not think of her stepmother any more.

She walked this way for a long time, but the light did not change; it seemed to always be morning. The sun continued its bright blinking overhead, and when shafts of golden light came through the leafy canopy, dust motes hung in the air, glittering as bright as diamonds. It was an enchantment, she was sure. This Wood was so gentle in comparison to the dark, thick forests near Rook Hill. There, the evergreens were so tall and so old she could not see the tops of them; here, oak and birch branches broke the sky into lacy filigrees of light green, exposing the tender blue above.

But at some point in her passage, the trees began to change. They stretched taller, and the soft, pale bark darkened, roughened. She put her hand to a tree and touched the lichen growing dark green upon brown, and it felt like old cork, dry and crumbling. Here the sun mellowed, took on the cast of late afternoon, and the shadows seemed to fall a bit longer; the forest had sunk into a deeper silence, magnifying what sounds did arise. The sudden, quick crash of a fox bounding through the brush was as loud as the slam of a great wooden door.

She came upon a bubbling stream, and she knelt down and dipped up a handful of icy water to drink. She gasped at the shocking cold of it. Wide, flat stones showed her the way across the streambed, and she stepped across carefully to avoid falling into the water. On the other side of the stream the Wood transformed into the dark forest she had known as a child: peeling, soft brown bark on the trees, and leaves like drooping feathers. The sky seemed to retreat far above, and she had the strange sensation that she was shrinking, that soon she might be no larger than an ant crawling over the ground. Here the Wood was a secret place, and she knew she was trespassing. But she went on, because she could not go back.

The path had narrowed; it was no longer the wide highway used by hunting parties. Instead, tree roots crossed the path, half-hidden by the mossy undergrowth. She passed young saplings clustering around the bases of the tallest trees like children surrounding their mother. She felt an old peace there, and something in the air that smelled like magic. When the path shrank to an uneven track that she could barely see in the deepening dusk, she felt a part of her heart sink into place: This was where she should go. It felt like home. The gathering darkness, the rise and fall of the ground, the giant, silent trees around her like columns supporting the vanishing sky – all of it was familiar. And soon the path became clear again: It was narrow but hard-trodden, and the trees parted from it willingly. In the distance she could see the edge of the Wood, some kind of building outlined in dim light, and perhaps a hill. She felt a faint prickling on the back of her neck, as if she had been to that place before. The ground descended in a slope towards the edge of the Wood, and when she approached the downhill portion, she knew where she was.

She stepped out of the Wood into the shadow of the hawthorn tree, and looked up the hill at the house where she had grown up. The windows were dark and empty.

She went to the tombstone that marked where her mother lay buried and knelt down on the new grass before it. She felt tears well up in her eyes and let them fall down her cheeks. She touched the stone marker, feeling the imprint of her mother's name with her fingers. And then she lay down, pressing her cheek against the edge of the stone where it met the soft ground, and closed her eyes.

She slept on the earth over her mother's grave, and she did not dream.

When she awoke it was dark, and the night air was cool against her skin. She was lying with her belly to the ground, breathing in the scent of the soil. She could feel the steady beating of her heart, the rhythmic pulsing of her blood through her veins, and beneath her the dense, solid earth. She rolled over onto her back and looked up through the branches of the tree, the new leaves a dark pattern against the black night sky. She wondered if Anya would be awake still, at her daughter's house in Rook Hill. She wondered if Anya would send her back to her stepmother. With that thought she woke up completely, the memory of the last several months flooding back into her with depressing efficiency. She sat up slowly and brushed the dirt from her hair.

Opposite her, a man was sitting on a rock. A thrill of fear coursed through her body, for there was something odd about him. First of all, there had never been a rock there before, and second, the man did not look exactly human either. He was dressed like a man, but a very exotic one. He wore white breeches and boots and a white shirt with white lace at the throat, and the fabric of his clothes gleamed as if there were light trapped within its threads. And then there was his face, which on first glance was just like a man's face, except that his skin was as white as his clothes, and his cheekbones were sharp as blades. Though his hair was pale as snow, he did not look old; he looked, in fact, like he had no age at all. His eyes glowed unnaturally blue, and when he opened his mouth to speak, she saw his skin sliding over the bones of his skull.

'What are you seeking?' he said, and his voice was silky and cold. Though they were separated by several feet, she was disconcerted by the intensity of his gaze; she felt as if he could pull her open from afar.

She answered, 'I came to see my mother.'

His eyes moved to the gravestone and then back to her face. An expression of some sort passed over his features, but she did not recognize it. He said, 'Come closer.'

She was compelled to get up; her muscles would not obey her own commands; and when she was standing before him she trembled from fear. She wanted to look away, but she could not turn her eyes away from his. They were cool, measuring, as faceted as finely cut jewels; they travelled over her face methodically, cataloguing her eyelashes, her nose, her mouth, her chin. He reached out and stroked her hair, and she could feel an icy chill emanating from his hand. She wondered if his touch would spread a frost over her, snowflakes blooming over her skin like a dress of winter. When he took her hand in his and ran his thumb down the center of her palm, the blood in her veins seemed to freeze. The pain of it freed her voice from her throat and she managed to ask, 'Are you the one who sent me back, that night?'

He looked back at her face, and she swallowed. For a moment he did not speak, and then he said, 'There are many of us.'

'Who are you?' she asked, her heart thudding in her chest.

'You know,' he said, 'who we are.'

She felt like a fool, but she pressed on. 'I wish to see my mother,' she said, and her voice shook.

'Your mother is dead,' he said.

'Can you not bring her back?' she asked desperately.

He let go of her hand and warmth rushed back into her fingers, making them ache. 'You dare to ask for such a great gift,' he said, and there was a note of amusement in his voice.

'Please,' she begged.

But he said coldly, 'No.'

Her stomach fell, and she whispered, 'Are you going to kill me?'

At first she thought that he might strike her down where she stood, for a look of ravenous hunger came over him, as if he could not wait to spill her blood. But as her heart hammered in her throat and cold sweat dampened her skin, he seemed to change his mind, and the expression on his angular face smoothed out until he was as unreadable as before. He stood up, towering over her, and said, 'You must go back the way you came. You took an enchanted path, and you cannot remain here.'

'Go back?' she repeated, and she was flooded with disappointment. 'Don't make me go back,' she pleaded.

'You have no choice in the matter,' he said curtly. He

turned, lifting his head as if he were listening for something she could not hear, and he said, 'I will take you there.'

And then a tall white stallion with golden eyes came out of the Wood towards them. In one smooth motion, the man picked her up and lifted her onto the saddle, and then he mounted behind her. She sat stiffly, afraid to lean back against him. The horse beneath her felt powerful and wild, but he moved so smoothly that Ash found herself relaxing against her will. As they glided through the dark trees, the texture of the air seemed to change – as if space were being compressed on their journey, and when she inhaled, it was like a gust of wind thrust down her throat. She could smell the scent of night-blooming jasmine and something indefinable – perhaps it was the smell of magic. Her head fell back against the man's shoulder, and soon her eyes drifted shut. She dreamed of gardens full of white roses, their perfume intoxicating. Above them a city of white stone towers – so tall she could not see their rooftops – rose to the blue sky.

When the horse slowed down she blinked her eyes open, and they were crossing the meadow. She saw Quinn House ahead, a single light burning in Lady Isobel's window. She sat up, pulling herself away from the man self-consciously. When they stopped outside the garden gate she tried to dismount hastily and he had to catch her hand, wrenching her arm back painfully, to prevent her from falling. When her feet touched the ground her knees almost buckled, and she grabbed at the horse's mane for balance, her other hand still held firmly in his grasp. 'You must not take that path again,' he said to her. She looked up at him, and here in the ordinary darkness, he seemed to have lost some of his otherworldly glow. 'Do you hear me?' he demanded.

'Yes,' she said quickly, afraid to upset him. He dropped her hand then, and she felt momentarily unbalanced. He turned the horse back towards the Wood, and within the blink of an eye they had vanished and Ash was left alone outside the garden gate.

Feeling as though she were fighting her way back through a fog of some sort, she reached for the gate to steady herself. She took a deep breath and realized that she was cold and hungry, for she had not eaten all day. She opened the gate and made her way back inside the house on shaking legs.

She was looking for the end of a loaf of bread when she heard footsteps come down the stairs and saw a light coming closer to the kitchen door. Lady Isobel soon appeared in the doorway, holding a candle in her hand.

'So you decided to come back after all, did you?' her stepmother said. 'Where have you been all day?'

Ash turned to her stepmother, backing up against the edge of the countertop. 'I just went for a walk and I got lost,' she said, trying to sound unruffled.

'Who told you that you could leave the house?' Lady Isobel demanded.

Ash hesitated. 'I didn't think I would be gone for long,' she finally said.

'You're a liar,' her stepmother said. 'Come here, Aisling.' She held out her hand.

'Can I – can I just go to bed?' she asked as her stomach growled loudly in protest.

The candlelight beneath Lady Isobel's face made her look like a monster. Her lip curled in anger and she said, 'You have been absent all day and you expect no punishment? Come here!'

'No,' Ash said impulsively, and then she knew she had made a mistake.

Lady Isobel came toward her and grabbed her upper arm in a fierce grip. Ash let out a gasp of pain as her stepmother propelled her back to the kitchen door.

'You are given entirely too much freedom,' she said as she opened the door and shoved Ash out into the yard. 'You shirk your duties on purpose and leave your work for others to do. You disrespect me and what I do for you.' Ash stumbled as she was pushed towards the corner of the house where the entrance to the cellar was sunk into the ground.

Ash struggled in her stepmother's grip, trying to twist away from her. 'Let me go!' she shouted.

'Be quiet!' her stepmother said angrily. She pushed Ash down the stone steps and followed close on her heels. She drew out a large black key from the pocket of her skirt and unlocked the cellar door, a massive block of thick oak. It creaked on its hinges as she threw it open. 'Get in there,' she commanded, and pushed Ash into the dark. 'And think about what trouble you've caused. I feed you and house you and you repay me by running off without a thought for your duties.' Her stepmother paused for a moment in the dark doorway, and Ash thought she could make out a faint smile on the woman's face. 'You are a shame to your father,' she said.

And then she stepped back out of the cellar and slammed the door shut, leaving Ash in the dark. The great iron key turned in the lock, and Ash heard her stepmother's footsteps receding until there was nothing but the muffled hum of the dark, and the cold, damp press of the cellar air against her skin.

7

Ash could hear her breath in the dark: quick, frightened, like a rabbit fleeing from hunting hounds. She put her hands out in front of herself and felt only cold air. She took a tentative step towards the door, shuffling forward until the tips of her fingers bumped against the wood. It was slightly wet. She flattened her palms against the door and then pressed her body to the oak. When she closed her eyes the quality of the dark did not change, and for a moment she stopped breathing, afraid that she could not tell if her eyes were open or shut. She touched her face, her eyelids, and the trembling movement of her eyes somehow reassured her: She was still real. Then she slid down to the ground, her face pressed against the door, her boots dragging roughly across the dirt floor. She gathered her knees to her chest to make herself as small as possible, and tried to ignore the weight of the darkness on her.

She must have fallen asleep, her cheek leaning against the door, because she thought she saw someone sitting next to her, and she thought it was her mother. The woman put her arm around Ash, and Ash dropped her head on to her mother's shoulder, felt the pressure of her mother's chin on her forehead. Her mother stroked her hair and said, 'Don't worry, Ash, I'm here.'

Ash felt the soft collar of her mother's blouse beneath her cheek. She slipped her arms around her mother's waist and pressed up close to her, feeling the solid warmth of her body. 'Don't go away again, Mother,' she whispered. 'I've missed you.'

'Shh,' her mother said. 'I know. You should rest now. You've been out all day and you're hungry.'

Ash could smell the scent of her mother's skin now, and it was the fragrance of the Wood, oak and moss and wildflower. She felt the dull thump of her mother's heartbeat, the lightness of her mother's breath on her hair, the gentle touch of her mother's hands stroking down the length of her back. The rhythm was echoed in the sound of her mother's fingers on the fabric of her dress, a subtle swoosh in the dark, up and down, up and down, the friction like a rope binding them together. Her mother pressed a kiss to her forehead, and her lips were warm.

When Ash opened her eyes, she could see. The cellar door was outlined with daylight, and it illuminated, dimly, bushels of potatoes and apples, sacks of flour and grain. Three trunks were stacked against the far wall;

there was an old wheelbarrow, garden tools, a coil of rope. She wrapped her arms around herself and felt the chill of the early morning.

She did not know how long she sat there before she heard footsteps above her. She realized she must be sitting beneath the kitchen floor. The footsteps moved away, and then the kitchen door slammed. At last the steps came down to the cellar door, and a key rattled in the lock. She scurried away from the door and was standing when it opened. She blinked in the sudden glare at the wide, dark shadow looming outside. A keyring dangled from the woman's hand, and when she spoke, Ash realized that it was Beatrice.

'It's time to make breakfast,' Beatrice said, as if she were accustomed to letting Ash out of the cellar every morning. 'Come outside; there's work to do.'

Ash followed her back into the world.

For months afterwards, Lady Isobel did not allow Ash to leave the house unaccompanied; she could not even go to the market without Beatrice keeping a hawk eye on her. At night, her stepmother followed her to her room and locked her in from the outside, and in the morning Beatrice let her out so that she could lay the fires and set the table for breakfast. At the end of the day, she would sit at her window and stare out at the Wood until the daylight was gone. She couldn't stop thinking about the path she had taken to Rook Hill. She often thought of the grave that waited at the end of it, and if she closed her eyes she could remember the smell of the earth there. She also remembered the fairy who had been waiting for her — for surely he could not have been human, could he? In all the fairy tales she had read, the fairies were described as unnaturally beautiful, and now Ash knew what that meant. There had been more to his beauty than perfect features: He radiated an allure that would be nearly impossible to resist.

Each night before she went to sleep, she chose one fairy tale to read until the light of her candle stub died. Her favorite story was of Kathleen, a pretty girl of sixteen who was betrothed to the village baker's son, a handsome young man with jet-black hair and smiling brown eyes. On her way home from his family's house one warm summer night, Kathleen, full of the heady rush of first love, lost herself in the Wood. In the distance she saw the twinkling of lights and mistakenly thought that it marked a villager's house — but it marked the edge of a fairy ring. That night, the story goes, the fairies were dressed in their finest, for it was Midsummer's Eve. The young Kathleen knew that she should not enter the ring, but there was a fairy prince there with eyes as brilliant as sapphires and a smile that drove away all thoughts of the baker's son. This fairy prince, who saw Kathleen standing outside the ring, took her hand and pulled her in, and then she was truly lost, for once anyone experiences a fairy's charm, nothing else, they say, will ever be enough.

Kathleen awoke the next morning in her own bed in her ordinary house, and she longed to be back in that fairy ring so much that her body ached with the memory of it. She ran to the village greenwitch and begged for something to help her find that place again, and the greenwitch – who was old enough to know better – gave Kathleen a wreath of mugwort and told her to burn three leaves every night before she went to bed so that she might dream of that land. Kathleen waited breathlessly all day for night to fall, and when darkness came she plucked the leaves from the wreath and set them afire in a small dish at the foot of her bed. The smoke curled up with a bittersweet odour, and soon she fell asleep and dreamt that she was back in the fairy ring. In her dreams she danced with the beautiful prince, who fed her the most delicious foods she had ever tasted and bestowed one kiss upon her lips every night.

As the days went by, Kathleen began to waste away, for she only truly lived when she slept at night, entombed in the prison of smoke from the magical wreath. Although the baker's son tried to woo her, she was no longer interested. Her mother plied her with the best food she could make, but Kathleen would not eat. Her friends tried to amuse her with funny tales, but she did not listen. On the night that she burned the wreath's last leaf, she did not come back from that dream world.

When her mother came to wake her the next morning, Kathleen would not open her eyes, though her breast still rose and fell, breathing in the lingering smoke from the burning wreath. They say that she did not die; instead she simply slept there, her mind lost, her body still and empty, alone on her narrow bed.

Ash read and re-read the story as if it were a map to her own future. Though she knew it was meant to be a cautionary tale, now that she had seen that fairy, she thought that Kathleen's fate was not so cruel after all.

When autumn came, Ash's stepmother told her to bring out the trunks of winter clothes stored under the stairs, and as she rummaged through the dusty, dark space, she came across a box of books that had been her father's. Kneeling near the lamp, Ash pulled out volumes on history and trade regulations, old account books, and a small, cloth-bound journal written in a fine hand. Inside the front cover her mother's name was written, and it was dated years before Ash had been born. She stuffed the book into her apron pocket, and all that day she felt the weight of it on her hip like hidden treasure. That night, squinting at the book in the candlelight, Ash saw that it contained what appeared to be recipes for medicines – or possibly spells. There was a remedy for fever; there was a recipe for alleviation of headache; there were instructions on making an ointment to treat burns. Under a long list of herbs, there was a notation next to the entry for mugwort: '*May be used sparingly for lucid dreams.*'

On one page titled '*To Reverse Glamour,*' many lines were crossed out, and the ink had been smeared and blotted several times as if her mother had been trying different combinations. '*Take one part feverfew,*' read the instructions, '*and mash with two thimblefuls of spring dew. Soak for one fortnight in a black glass bottle beneath the shade of a mature hawthorn tree. Add one part wilted bryony stem, brewed with essence of verbena in cotter's wine. If necessary, add foxglove.*' At the bottom of the page was a note: '*Maire Solanya believes ineffective. Will test on next full moon.*'

There were several pages of notes on love, and Ash wondered if it were an attempt at a love potion, but there were few ingredients. One line was underscored several times: '*The knowledge will change him.*' But though Ash paged through the entire journal, she never found out who he was.

One morning in early winter, Beatrice did not come to unlock her door. Instead her stepmother turned the key in the lock and woke her, saying, 'Beatrice is ill. She won't be here today.' When Ash went downstairs, Beatrice was not in her quarters behind the kitchen. 'She went to her daughter's to recover,' Lady Isobel said when Ash asked where she had gone.

But she did not come back the next day, or the next

one. At night, after Ash had washed the supper dishes and banked the kitchen fire, her stepmother called for her to come to her chamber. 'It's time for you to start learning something beyond scrubbing the floor,' said her stepmother, and held out her hairbrush.

'But Beatrice does this,' Ash said in surprise.

'Beatrice is not coming back,' said Lady Isobel.

'What happened?' Ash asked, startled. 'Is she all right?'

'She is fine,' her stepmother said. 'But I can no longer afford to keep Beatrice on here, so you will be required to take over her duties.'

'But there is too much work even for two,' Ash objected.

'Then you will have to learn how to work harder,' said Lady Isobel, holding the hairbrush out pointedly. When Ash did not move to take it, her stepmother continued, 'You already know who to blame for this: your father. If he had not left so many debts, you might have had a lady's upbringing. But the best you can hope for now, Aisling, is to be a lady's maid.'

Ash flushed with anger. 'I will not —' she began, but her stepmother interrupted her.

'You are not the only one who must sacrifice. I hope that Ana and Clara's future will not be shortchanged because of your father's debts. And if you run away, you will not only be confirming the fact that your father was a selfish man who did nothing more than take my money before he died, you will be at the mercy of whomever finds you wandering out there on the King's Road.' Lady Isobel asked in a silky voice, 'Do you know what happens to girls who are found wandering about without protection?'

Ash reluctantly closed her fingers around the hairbrush and raised it to her stepmother's head. She began to brush Lady Isobel's thick hair with short, rough strokes. A small smile twisted her stepmother's lips as Ash yanked the hairbrush down, pulling out strands of auburn hair. Her stepmother reached up and grasped Ash's right wrist in a bruising grip and said, 'Careful, now. Is that any way to treat your mistress?'

The next morning, Ash moved her belongings into the room next to the kitchen where Beatrice had once slept. There was no brazier in the room, so it was the coldest in the house, but Ash did not mind the chill. Now that Beatrice was gone, there was nobody to unlock her door in the mornings, which meant that Lady Isobel could not lock her in at night, either. At first Ash thought that she would go immediately into the Wood at night – she wanted to find that fairy again. But doing Beatrice's work as well as her own left her exhausted. At the end of the day, all she wanted to do was lean against the warm kitchen hearth, reading, the soot smearing down the length of her skirt. And just as she became more adept at her work, the winter came in earnest.

It snowed earlier and more heavily than it had in years, and the roads were often impassable. Yule was a subdued affair, for the King and his eldest son were away on a military campaign far in the south, and because of the harsh weather the hunting season ended earlier than usual. So by the time she was able to return to the Wood, stealing out of Quinn House on the first night the chill lessened, it had been almost a year since she had walked back to her mother's grave. This time, as she wrapped herself in her old cloak and let herself out of the house, she knew what she was seeking, and it made her pulse quicken in anticipation.

When she reached the forest, she hoped that she could find the path she had followed the year before. But although she walked and walked, she did not find it, and as she went farther into the trees the ground became more and more overgrown, so that soon she was picking her way over tree roots and grasping low-hanging branches to keep her balance. Once she tripped and fell, and a sharp stick reared up like a claw at her cheek. She put her finger to her face and to her surprise felt a warm, wet smear, and in the dim light she saw the dark shade of blood on her fingertips.

The night was growing colder, and when a gust of wind blew past her she remembered that it was, after all, barely spring, and the ground beneath her was still frozen, the hollows still dusted with snow. It was dangerous weather; she could freeze to death. Yet she went on with a kind of feverish urgency, driven by a fierce need to go deeper into the Wood. She could feel something calling to her, and that should have been a warning, but she only felt reassured by it: She was going in the right direction. She went on until her feet grew numb from the cold, and at last she found what she had been looking for. There, sitting on a fallen log as if he had been waiting for her, was the fairy who had taken her back to Quinn House last spring.

She went to him, her heart pounding, and knelt down on the ground, pushing back her hood. 'I came to find you,' she said, looking up at him. His face was strangely disturbing, his skin like the surface of a pond, but it was also more beautiful than she remembered.

He raised one hand to her face and his fingers curved over the gash in her cheek; it burst into fiery pain at his touch. 'You are bleeding,' he said, and rubbed a smear of her blood between his fingers. The sight of her blood on his pale skin made her shudder, and yet she felt herself lean toward him instinctively, wanting to close the space between them.

She said: 'Once my mother told me a story: There was a girl whose parents died in an accident, and every night the girl visited her parents' grave and laid flowers upon it. But one twilight, as she was sitting at the grave, a rider came to the girl.' As she spoke she saw his eyes grow calmer, as if her words were soothing him. She continued: 'He was the handsomest man she had ever seen, dressed all in white with a horse as white as snow, and he told her that she should come with him to see her parents. She was so eager to see them again that she agreed, and when the man offered her his hand she took it, and it was as cold as death. He put her on his horse and took her away, and she was never seen again, for he had been one of the riders of the Fairy Hunt.'

When she stopped speaking he said nothing for a moment, and Ash realized that all of the Wood was silent around them – she could not even hear the sound of the wind in the branches, though she felt its cold breath on her face.

Finally he said, 'Is that why you sought me out? To tell me a—' He paused, his lip curling, and continued, 'A *fairy* tale?'

She was undaunted. 'Is it true?' she asked. 'Is the tale true?'

'What is true for your people is not true for mine,' he answered.

'But can you not take me to see her?' she asked, and she yearned for him to say yes.

'Your mother is dead, Aisling,' he said, and the words felt like they were physically striking her.

She took his cold hands in hers, and she insisted, 'She cannot be. I have felt her spirit alive. I know I have.'

For a moment as they looked at each other, she thought she saw him wrestle with what to say, but then the hardness returned to his eyes and he said curtly, 'You must go home.'

He stood up, letting go of her hands. She scrambled up as well and said, 'You know my name. What is yours?'

He hesitated, but at last said, 'You may call me Sidhean.'

She tried it out: 'Sidhean.' The sound of it was foreign and exotic to her.

He seemed to recoil from the sound of his name on her tongue. 'You must go home,' he said again.

'Why?' she asked, and feeling reckless, she added, 'Take me with you.'

'It is not time yet,' he said. In the word *yet*, she heard a promise, and it flooded her with hope.

He held his hand out to her, and when she took it he pulled her close, wrapping them both inside his cloak. Just before her eyes closed, she realized she could hear his heartbeat beneath her ear, as quick as her own.

When she woke up, she was lying in her bed at Quinn House, a thick, silvery-white cloak thrown over her. She sat up, dazed, pushing the cloak aside; it was softer than any velvet or leather she had ever touched. She climbed out of bed and opened the shutters, and in the early morning light she marvelled at the sheer beauty of the thing. It was made of some kind of fur that rippled like multi-coloured scales or iridescent feathers. It *was* white, but when she looked at it sideways it seemed to glow, and sometimes it shone like polished silver. She picked it up and wrapped it around herself, the weight of it comforting and solid. *This is real*, she thought, and a shiver went down her spine, for that meant that Sidhean – and all of his world – was real, too.

8

As the years passed, Ash came to know the many trails in the King's Forest very well. She often walked there at night, the fairy cloak like a ghost around her shoulders, but she did not seek out the path to Rook Hill. As the Wood became familiar to her, she became attuned to the sounds it made: the light tread of deer, the rustling leaves, the flapping passage of night owls. Sometimes she heard footsteps behind her, but she rarely saw where they came from. Once she caught sight of Sidhean out of the corner of her eye; he was standing perhaps twenty feet to her left, but when she turned to look, he was gone. She came to recognize the slight prickling on her skin that signalled he was nearby. It felt like someone running a finger down the back of her spine.

The first night that he allowed her to walk with him, her entire body was tense with excitement; she was afraid to speak in case he disappeared again. That night everything looked different: Nothing seemed solid.

Every tree, every stone, was merely a shadow. She felt like she would be able to walk through walls if Sidhean were with her. Once in late spring she watched a doe and two speckled fawns come out of the shadows to bow down to him, and when he placed his hands on the heads of those two fawns, Ash said in wonder, 'They do not fear you.'

'We do not hunt them,' he said simply. He did not seem to mind if she asked him about the animals in the Wood, but if she asked him about his people, he would answer in a low growl, 'You know I cannot tell you.'

'If I am to be among your kind,' she said once, 'should I not know about them?'

That made him angry, and she did not see him for many weeks after that. When he finally returned, she was careful to speak only of unimportant things, for while he had been gone she discovered, to her surprise, that she missed him. In this way they developed a kind of unspoken agreement: He would accompany her, and she would not ask him about who he was. If it occurred to her that her friendship – if that is what it was – with this fairy was a little strange, she did not dwell on it, for it was the only companionship she had, and she did not want to lose it.

After Ana's sixteenth birthday, Lady Isobel began to regularly take her daughters to visit her sister in the City, for it was time to introduce Ana to society. Each visit was presaged by trips to the seamstress to fit a new dress or disguise an old one, and each time they returned there was fresh news about the royal court. Even Clara, who had never before been interested in such things, began to talk about Prince Aidan, who was in the far south leading a military campaign.

'He must be so handsome,' Clara said, sitting on the edge of Ana's bed while Ash finished braiding Ana's hair.

'You have never even seen him,' Ana said dismissively.

'You haven't either,' Clara objected.

'I have seen a painting,' Ana said, 'in the parlor of Lady Margaret's townhouse, and he is indeed handsome.'

Clara clasped her hands together and asked eagerly, 'Do you think we will meet him soon?'

Ana laughed. 'Sister, you cannot be harbouring a secret love for the prince, can you?' Clara blushed. 'Because you would never suit him, Clara,' Ana continued. 'You are too young, too unrefined.' And Ana gave herself a smug smile in the mirror. Clara looked downfallen, and Ash could not resist pulling a bit too hard on Ana's hair while she tied a ribbon on the end. 'Ouch!' Ana cried, putting a hand to her head. 'Be careful, Ash. You're so clumsy – why do you think we never bring you with us to the City? It would be an embarrassment.'

'I am sorry, Stepsister,' Ash said contritely, but the words tasted bitter. 'I shall endeavour to be less clumsy.'

Ana seemed mollified. 'Well, try a bit harder, and

perhaps one day you'll be allowed to come with us.'

But Ash was more than happy to be left behind. While they were gone, Ash took her books into the Wood and walked until she found a sunny bit of riverbank, where she spread out her cloak and lay down, propped up on her elbows, to read.

In the autumn when hunting season began, sometimes she heard the hunters riding by, and she would lie very still, wondering if the dogs would find her. One late afternoon when the sun was spreading honey-gold over the trees, Ash lay on the riverbank beneath an old oak whose limbs grew nearly down to the ground to form a splendid, secret room. She had been reading an old fairy tale that afternoon, and when she finished the story, she looked up through the leaves across the river and saw a woman there. She was kneeling on the edge of the opposite bank with a dripping hand raised halfway to her mouth, and she was dressed in hunting gear. The woman drank from the water in her hand and then flicked the rest away, the droplets scattering like crystals in the slanting light, and when she looked up she saw Ash staring at her. Before Ash had a chance to hide there was a shout in the distance and the woman glanced in the direction of the sound. She looked back at Ash and smiled at her, then rose to her feet and walked away, her tread so light that Ash couldn't hear it.

Ash let out her breath in relief and lay down on her

back, staring up at the arching branches. The sky peeked through the leaves in brilliant blue, and she could smell the rich scent of the earth beneath her: crushed leaves from last fall, acorns slowly decaying into soil. She wondered if the woman was the huntress who led the hunting party she had heard in the Wood that morning, their bugles ringing. She closed her eyes, feeling the peace of the afternoon on her skin, the warm breath of the air and the solid mass of the ground beneath her, and she fell asleep. She dreamed that she was perched on a boulder overlooking a twisting path in the heart of the Wood, and below her she saw the huntress walking. When the woman stopped and knelt to examine something on the ground, Ash climbed down from the rocky outcropping and dropped on to the path. The huntress looked up at Ash with eyes the colour of spring leaves and said, 'You've found me.'

Ash woke up suddenly and scrambled onto her knees, blinking rapidly. The sun was gone and night had stripped the colour from the trees, and she was going to be late getting home. She quickly pocketed her book, pulled the cloak around her shoulders, and shoved her way out of the overhanging branches, nearly running towards the path that would take her back to Quinn House.

The winter that Ana turned eighteen, Prince Aidan and his soldiers returned home at last from a successful five-year campaign in the south. Soon afterwards, the King announced a grand celebration in the City during Yule that winter, and Lady Isobel was overjoyed, for Ana was well ready to find a husband. 'Isn't it fortuitous,' Lady Isobel gloated one night at supper, 'that the prince has returned just in time to meet my most beautiful daughter?'

Ana smiled at her mother, and Ash thought her stepsister might have looked pretty then, lit by the glowing candles, were it not for the greed in her eyes. 'I must have new gowns for the balls,' Ana said fervently. 'I must look like a princess!'

Lady Isobel reached out and stroked her daughter's cheek, answering, 'No, my dear, you must look like a *queen*.' Ana giggled then, a high-pitched squeal that startled Ash into nearly dropping the heavy soup tureen she was removing from the dining table. Her stepmother saw her fumble and said sharply, 'Watch what you're doing, Aisling. I won't have you destroying my dishes.'

'I am sorry, Stepmother,' Ash said, gritting her teeth. 'I slipped.'

'Take care that you don't slip again,' Lady Isobel said. 'Particularly when we go to Yule – you'll be coming with us as Ana's lady's maid.'

Ash paused, still holding the soup tureen, and stared at her stepmother in surprise. 'But you've never taken me with you when you visit the City,' she said.

'Then be thankful,' Lady Isobel said curtly. 'Goodness

knows what you're up to when we leave you here. You need to see something of society if you're ever going to work in any other household. Just be sure to hold your tongue.' When Ash continued to stare at her, dumbfounded, Lady Isobel said, 'What are you standing there for? Get on with your work.'

Ash spent the week before their trip to the City preparing Ana's newest gowns, packing and unpacking the trunks as Ana changed her mind about what to bring, and listening to Ana's and Clara's excited chatter about the possibility of meeting Prince Aidan.

'Perhaps we'll have an audience with him,' Clara said as she sorted through a pile of laces while Ash and Lady Isobel organized Ana's gowns.

'Lady Margaret knows the prince's chancellor,' Ana said, 'and she told me I should be prepared for the opportunity at the Yule ball.'

Lady Isobel said, 'Yes, you must be prepared — you will only have an instant to make him notice you.'

'Of course I shall be ready, Mother,' Ana said, tossing her head as if the task was no more difficult than selecting which dress to wear on the appointed evening. But Ash detected an undercurrent of anxiety in her stepsister, and she could not help it — she began to feel sorry for her. Even Ana was not immune from Lady Isobel's demands, and Ash was glad that she only had to keep the house clean, not find a husband.

When the day of their departure finally arrived, Ash rose early to drag the trunks out to the hired carriage, only to have to repack Ana's one last time when her stepsister decided to take her black fur stole after all. By the time the carriage was fully packed and her stepmother and stepsisters were sitting within, Ash was tired and wished she were being left behind after all. She was not sure if she could endure another week of Ana's nervous pursuit of a husband. Her mood showed plainly on her face, for when she climbed up next to the driver, Jonas, he gave her a wry grin and said, 'Cheer up, Aisling. At least you won't be alone for Yule.'

'I'd rather be alone,' Ash snapped.

He laughed at her. 'Would you really?' He picked up the reins and urged the horses forward, their bridles jangling. She crossed her arms and huddled into her cloak, refusing to answer, watching her breath steaming out into the cold winter air.

As they drove away from Quinn House, the morning cloud cover began to clear, and by the time they left the village behind, the sun shone brightly down on the road. The most recent snowfall was churned up in clumps beneath the horses' hooves, but it lay along the fields in a pristine, sparkling white blanket. Ash shifted uncomfortably on the hard wooden seat, and as she pulled back the hood of her cloak to look up at the blue sky, she heard hunting horns in the distance. She couldn't see the hunting party, though, until they turned onto the hard-packed King's Highway, and then at first she could only see flashes of colour in the distance that might be the red and blue of the King's pennant. When at last she could pick out the individual riders, she saw bay and black and chestnut hunting horses, and when she could see the face of the pennant-bearer – a sandy-haired boy in blue livery – Jonas pulled their carriage to the side of the road to let the hunt pass.

Behind the pennant-bearer a woman rode a bay mare with a black forelock, one hand resting on the pommel of her saddle and the other holding the reins; the hood of her deep blue cloak was flung back and she was laughing with the rider next to her. Ash realized with a jolt of surprise that this was the woman she had seen in the Wood that autumn afternoon. Ash twisted around in her seat to watch her ride past, and asked Jonas, 'Is that the King's Huntress?'

'I believe so,' he answered.

'She is young,' Ash said, remembering the story of Eilis and the Changeling.

'Yes. I believe she was only recently an apprentice herself.'

The dozen or so riders of the hunt passed them, with the sight hounds running lightly alongside. 'What happened to the previous huntress?' Ash asked.

Jonas shrugged. 'She may simply have moved on. They do, those women.'

After the last of the hunt's wagons passed, Jonas

pulled the carriage back onto the road, but Ash clung to the edge of the seat, looking back at them until they disappeared around the bend.

They reached the City gates just before noon and joined a line of carriages jostling their way up the hill into the Royal City for the Yule celebrations. Inside the City walls the merchants had decorated their shops with pine boughs and winterberries, and the bright sunlight reflected off freshly polished shop windows. They drove past a great square dotted with market stalls, and then Jonas turned down a quieter street lined with townhouses, driving slightly uphill. In the distance between the buildings she could sometimes see the white stone towers of the palace. Just as the sun came directly overhead, Jonas pulled onto a street flanked on both sides by houses grander than any that Ash had seen so far, and they stopped in front of a three-storey brick building hung with a huge wreath of holly and white winterberries.

'Here we are,' Jonas said, nodding at the house. 'Page Street.'

The front door was opened by a young woman in a maid's uniform, and then another woman – the mistress of the house – came outside behind her, dressed in a blue velvet gown with a white lace cap over her dark hair. Jonas climbed down and opened the carriage door, helping Lady Isobel out onto the cobblestones. Ash clambered down off the high driver's seat and started to untie the trunks from the rear of the carriage as Lady Isobel greeted her sister. The maid came to help Ash while Ana and Clara followed their mother and aunt indoors. 'You'll be staying in my room,' the maid said to her, grasping one handle of Ana's trunk and helping Ash to lift it off the footboard. 'My name is Gwen.'

'Thank you,' Ash said as they struggled with the heavy trunk. 'I'm Ash.'

'Welcome,' Gwen said with a quick smile, and they carried the trunk into the house and hefted it up the grand staircase. When they reached the room where Ana was to stay, it was so much grander than Ana's room in Quinn House that Ash simply stared for a moment, looking around, to catch her breath. The two tall windows were hung with dark-gold brocade, and the dressing table in the corner was carved out of rosewood, the slender legs ending in feet that looked like the talons of a gryphon. A porcelain vase etched in gold was placed on the bedside table and filled with a spray of fragrant evergreen.

'Ash, are you coming?' Gwen asked, and Ash saw the girl standing expectantly in the doorway. 'I think there are more trunks to bring up.'

Embarrassed at her wide-eyed gawking, Ash answered, 'Yes, I'm sorry.' But the afternoon passed too quickly for Ash to dwell on the differences between Quinn House and this one. She had to unpack for Ana and Clara and Lady Isobel, press their gowns for the evening ahead, and brush off their travelling cloaks. That afternoon she spent a tedious hour assisting Ana in dressing for dinner, and in the evening the house was full of ladies in rich satin gowns and gentlemen wearing plush velvet and shining boots. The sight of them in all their finery reminded her of Yule in Rook Hill. One year her mother had made her a fairy costume to wear, and Ash still remembered the smile on her mother's face as she brushed silver paint onto Ash's cheeks.

'You'll be the prettiest fairy there,' her mother had told her, and Ash grinned as her mother tucked a cloak of white rabbit fur around her chin.

'Do you think we'll see any real fairies?' Ash had asked excitedly.

'Perhaps,' her mother had answered, dipping her brush back into the pot of silver paint.

'How will I recognize them?'

'Sometimes they dress as ordinary humans,' her mother replied, trailing the tip of the brush over her daughter's skin.

'Why?'

'At Yule we all dress as someone we are not,' her mother explained. 'It is tradition.'

'And the fairies follow our traditions?' Ash asked.

Her mother laughed. 'Perhaps it is we who follow theirs.'

'But how will I know if I see a fairy?' Ash asked

again. 'If they look like ordinary people, I won't be able to tell.'

'You'll be able to tell,' her mother told her, 'because wherever they touch, they'll leave a bit of gold dust behind.' She put down the brush and turned her daughter to face the mirror. 'Now look – there's the prettiest fairy I've ever seen.' Ash stared at herself, spellbound. Her eyes had been outlined in silver paint, and the color trailed down her cheeks in wondrous curls of gleaming light.

'It is like magic,' Ash whispered.

Her mother smiled at her, her hand touching her hair. 'Yes, my love, it is.'

That night, after all the guests had gone and all the remains of the party were cleared away, Ash was exhausted. But lying beside Gwen in her small attic chamber, she could not find a comfortable position on the straw ticking. She was afraid to move and disturb Gwen's rest, but she couldn't keep still and ended up pressing herself as close to the edge of the bed as possible.

She wondered whether Sidhean and his kind marked Yule in the same way that humans did. In all the stories she had read or heard, the fairies seemed to do nothing more than drink and dance, enjoying a life of leisure and frivolity. But Sidhean had always seemed, to Ash, to harbour an unexplained sadness. Why, if he and his kind were so content – if they celebrated Yule, so to speak, all year – why did he spend those nights walking with her? When they had first begun their unusual companionship, she had expected that he would soon do as all his kind were believed to do, and take her away with him. She was not sure what would await her on the other side, but she had wanted to know. Even an eternity serving him – especially him – seemed like no worse, and possibly much better, than a mere human lifetime serving Lady Isobel. Now, she no longer knew what he was planning to do. Why had he not claimed her already? What was he waiting for?

Lying awake in the City, Ash could hear Gwen's steady breathing in the dark, and she felt the distance between her and Sidhean for the first time, and it made her long for him. She turned over onto her side and closed her eyes, trying to force herself to sleep. But in her mind's eye all she could see was him, and she wanted to be with him, all of his cold strangeness. She wanted to take his hand, and she wanted him to pull her on to his horse, and they would go through the dark Wood at midnight, the moon a pale crescent above. They would ride to that crystal city where it is said that the fairies have their grandest palace, and she would know, at last, what Kathleen had known.

When Ash woke up, Gwen was still asleep, and the early dawn light was sliding through the gaps in the shutters over the dormer window. She gingerly eased herself out of bed to avoid waking Gwen, and dressed as quietly as possible. Tiptoeing down the stairs to the kitchen, she saw that the embers had burned low in the hearth and none of the servants was yet awake. She sat down on the warm hearthstones and put her head in her hands, feeling tired and disoriented. When the cook came into the kitchen an hour later, she found Ash asleep on the hearth, her head pillowed on her arms and her knees drawn close to her body, soot clinging to her dress.

9

The Yule celebrations that week were grander than anything Ash had ever experienced. Every night, Ash helped Ana dress for a different banquet or ball, and when her stepsister finally departed, she had to prepare the next night's gown. Her stepmother had spared no expense for her eldest daughter that year; there was a different gown for each night, and each one was more magnificent than the one before. It was disorienting for Ash, who was accustomed to the quiet of Quinn House; the bustling kitchen of the Page Street mansion and the number of servants going about their tasks were dizzying. Gwen had appointed herself Ash's guide for the week, and Gwen herself was like no other girl Ash had ever known. She was sweet, and prone to fits of the giggles, and blushed every time any young man said a word to her. In comparison, Ash felt clumsy and shy, and sometimes she caught herself staring at Gwen as if she were some kind of exotic bird about to take flight.

On the last night of Yule week there was a royal

masque held at the palace, where Prince Aidan would himself be attending. That afternoon Ana was in a mighty temper, complaining that Ash had forgotten the lace mantle that was to be worn over the purple velvet bodice, and when Ash found it wedged mysteriously behind the dressing table, Ana fumed that Ash was out to sabotage her. By the time Ana and the rest of the household departed in hired carriages for the masque, Ash was so frustrated with her stepsister that she felt certain she would have sabotaged her if the chance arose. But Ana managed to escape the house unscathed, and Ash watched the front door close on her velvet-and-feather-and-silk ensemble with relief. She sank down onto the bottom step of the staircase and was still sitting there a few minutes later when Gwen emerged from the dining room, a stack of clothes in her arms.

'What are you doing?' Gwen asked, her face flushed with excitement. 'It's almost time to go!'

'Go where?' Ash asked warily. 'Lady Isobel did not want me to attend them at the royal masque.'

Gwen laughed. 'Oh, not there – we're going to the City Square,' she explained, shaking out the clothes to reveal a pair of blue velvet breeches and a matching jacket. 'Did you bring your costume?'

Ash shook her head and said, 'No, I don't have anything like that.'

Gwen frowned. 'Well, you can't go in your maid's dress. We'll have to find something for you. Wait here,' she commanded, and went back into the dining room. She returned several minutes later with a slender young man whom Ash recognized as part of the household staff. Gwen said, 'This is Colin; he'll let you borrow his old liveries.' And then Gwen ran upstairs, shouting behind her, 'Hurry! We're all leaving in a quarter of an hour.'

Colin motioned for her to follow him. 'I'm in the back,' he said. She walked with him to the male servants' quarters at the rear of the house, where Colin's small, square room was found. His roommate, a tall, skinny boy who worked in the stable, was cocking a velvet cap onto his head and preening in front of the small mirror nailed to the back of the door. Colin opened the trunk at the foot of his bed and pulled out dark blue breeches and a white waistcoat, a white shirt with unfolded cravat, and a dark blue overcoat.

'These should fit you,' Colin said, piling the items into Ash's arms. 'They're too small for me now.'

'Thank you for letting me borrow them,' she said.

He straightened up, grinned at her, and said, 'You're welcome.'

They stood awkwardly together for a moment, and then Ash said, 'Well, I'd better go upstairs and get dressed.'

He nodded. 'We're meeting in the front hall.'

'All right then,' she mumbled, and backed out of the room.

Upstairs Gwen was tying her hair back, but even dressed as a boy, Gwen's figure was unmistakably feminine. She smiled at Ash and asked, 'Did Colin find something for you to wear?'

Ash nodded. 'Yes; he gave me these.' She set the clothing down on the bed and looked at the pile.

'Excellent; we'll be page boys together,' Gwen said, applying the finishing touches to her costume. 'If I can't go as a queen, I suppose this will have to do.' Finally satisfied with her appearance, she turned to leave the room, then paused and asked, 'Do you want me to help you?'

Ash shook her head. 'I'll be all right – go ahead and I'll meet you downstairs.'

'Ten minutes, not more,' Gwen reminded her, then left and pulled the door shut behind her.

When she was alone, Ash unbuttoned her dress and pulled it over her head, folding it carefully at the foot of the bed. She pulled off her petticoat and her shoes, and stood for a moment in the room in her camisole, her arms crossed over her chest, until she realized that the air was too chilly to be standing around undressed. It felt strange to be invited to go anywhere, and part of her just wanted to stay in Gwen's room alone and not have to talk to anyone. But Gwen had been so kind to her – an unexpected friend – that Ash did not want to disappoint her, so she pulled on the shirt and tucked it into the breeches. The fastenings were strange and felt backward, and the breeches were a little too large. She buttoned the waistcoat snugly over the shirt and sat down to lace on her boots, then pulled her hair back and tucked it beneath the high collar before tying the cravat around her neck. When she shrugged on the overcoat and went to look in the mirror, Ash saw someone else – a boy with a proud profile and dark, long-lashed eyes. Although Gwen had looked like the same girl wearing her brother's clothes, Ash looked like a stranger. And if she looked nothing like herself, she thought, then she couldn't possibly be herself. Perhaps her entire life – all her memories, thoughts, emotions – would melt away from her, leaving only the flesh-and-bone shell behind. She blinked at herself slowly, but in the mirror she looked the same: unrecognizable.

Downstairs the servants were laughing in the front hall. She could hear them as she walked down the back stairs, her hand sliding down the polished wooden banister. When she rounded the last corner, Gwen saw her and squealed. 'Look at Ash!' Gwen ran up the stairs to grab her hand and pull her down. 'You look magnificent,' she said, beaming.

Before she could reply, the butler began herding them out the door and into the wagon waiting in the courtyard. Squashed between the parlour maid dressed in riding leathers and the cook dressed as a king, Ash took the bottle of brandy they pressed into her hand and sipped at it, the bite of the liquid making her cough in surprise. They all laughed at her and patted her on the back, urging her to take another drink. By the time the wagon arrived at the Square, she felt pleasantly numb to the chill air. A massive bonfire was burning at the centre, which had been emptied of market stalls and was now filled with revellers in costumes of all colours and kinds. She caught glimpses of feathers and crooked paper crowns, rose-hued cheeks and deeply rouged lips, gowns of rich red and gold velvet. She followed the laughing crowd into the circle of dancers weaving their way around the crackling flames, and she let Colin spin her through unfamiliar steps, the Square a blur of colour in her eyes.

As they whirled around the bonfire she caught sight of the musicians with their pipes and drums, dressed like jokers in pointed caps with long gold tassels and jingling bells. When the pounding of the drums suddenly died, the dancers stopped in confusion, their applause abruptly ending, but then Ash heard a great cheer go up from the far side of the Square. She pushed through the crowd to see what was the cause of the noise, and saw a dozen riders entering the Square, the heads of their horses plumed with feathered headdresses that made them look like fantastic beasts, half horse, half eagle. The riders were dressed all in black with cloaks lined in shining white silk, and the revellers around Ash whispered excitedly to each other that it was the Royal Hunt, come to bestow the King's favours upon them.

As the horses made their way into the square, the riders reached into their saddlebags and threw out handfuls of sparkling gold coins, and the revellers cheered louder and clustered around the sleek horses, laughing and calling for more. Ash watched Gwen and Colin and the other household servants join the crowd around the Royal Hunt, but she remained where she was, the crackling heat of the bonfire at her back. The King's Huntress was in the middle of the group of riders, and she too was flinging out sparkling gold coins, and her horse's headdress was plumed in a crown of red feathers. When the hunters had given away all their gold, the huntress dismounted and led her riders towards the bonfire, where they joined hands with the revellers who flowed back around them, laughing and jostling for space near them, and the musicians struck up an infectious rhythm as the hunters' voices rose up in an old song:

> *Like blood and bone*
> *river and stone*
> *the Wood is field*
> *the stag brought home.*

Caught in the circle, Ash found herself whirled around the bonfire by strangers. Through the flames she could see the huntress singing, her face glowing in the red-gold light.

When the song ended, the hunters bowed to the gathered people and reclaimed their horses, then rode out of the square, the horses' hooves clattering loudly on the paving stones. Ash saw Gwen standing nearby and ran towards her, tugging on the girl's arm. 'Why are they leaving so soon?' she asked.

'They're going to the royal masque,' Gwen answered. 'They only come to give away the gold.' When Gwen saw the look of disappointment on Ash's face, she grinned. 'You like the hunters, do you? Have you fallen in love with one of them?' she teased her.

Ash blushed, but said, 'Of course not.'

Gwen laughed and took Ash's hand, leading her back to the dancers. 'Come, let's find you a handsome young lord for tonight.'

But soon Gwen became distracted by a handsome young lord of her own, and Ash excused herself from the dancing circle, feeling that she had had enough. She made her way out of the crowd toward the edge of the Square, where she stood with her back to a cold brick wall and watched the festivities. She could still see Colin and Gwen and the other members of the household staff dancing near the bonfire, their faces flushed with firelight and brandy. A young couple stumbled away from the dance hand in hand, one woman dressed in gold, the other woman in green, and Ash saw the smiles on their faces before they kissed. Another reveller, a laughing young boy wearing a joker's cap, came and pulled them back towards the dancers. Ash wondered suddenly if Ana and Clara were dancing with the hunters at the royal masque. In the distance she could see the pale spires of the palace, windows lit with hundreds of candles in the dark night, presiding over the merriment in the Square like a distant, decorous Fairy Queen. She wished she were there.

Feeling awkward and alone, Ash left the Square, walking back to where they had left the wagon on a side street. The horses, their breath making small clouds in the air, paid little attention to her as she climbed in. She pulled a lap blanket from beneath the seats and wrapped it around herself. She could still hear the music and laughter from the Square, but it was more muted here, and she found herself nodding off. She curled up on the hard wooden seat and fell asleep.

She was jolted awake by the sudden movement of the wagon beneath her as Gwen and Colin and the other household servants climbed onto the seats. She sat up, bleary-eyed, and asked, 'What's going on?'

'Time to go home,' said one of the servants, settling his considerable weight down with a sigh on one of the benches.

'And tend to her ladyship,' Gwen put in, looking out of breath but happy. They returned to an empty, dark house, and Ash and Gwen climbed the stairs to their attic room slowly, their feet heavy on the worn wooden floorboards. Ash took off Colin's clothes and folded them carefully on the lid of the trunk, and then put on her brown dress again, winding her hair into its customary knot at the nape of her neck. Just as she had finished, she heard the sound of carriages outside, and she went downstairs to meet Lady Isobel and her daughters in their rooms. They were chattering excitedly about the beautiful ladies and handsome lords they had seen that night, the magnificent spread that had been laid out on the silver-and-mahogany buffet in the great hall of the palace, and the skill of the musicians who had played such wonderful music.

As Ash began unwinding the ribbons from Ana's hair, Ana asked, 'Did you go with the servants tonight, Aisling? Mother said they normally have a bonfire in the City Square.'

Ash nodded. 'I did.'

'I'm surprised the King still allows such an old-fashioned spectacle,' Ana observed. 'But I suppose we must allow the servants some of their traditional comforts.' She caught Ash's eye in the mirror. 'It must have brought back memories for you – did you feel at home?' And then she gave Ash a pitying smirk. 'What am I saying? Rook Hill was such a small village; nothing in the City – even a superstitious Yule bonfire – is comparable.'

Feeling irritated, Ash forced herself to continue methodically untangling Ana's hair from the ribbons and pins. It had never done any good to allow Ana to goad her into an angry retort. Instead she asked, 'Did you meet the royal family?'

'Oh, yes,' Ana replied. 'I met His Royal Highness, of course. He is such a handsome man, and so kind as well. Mother thinks he was quite taken with me,' she said with a satisfied smile. Ash pulled out the last of the pins and began brusquely to brush Ana's hair. 'Gently!' Ana commanded. 'Haven't I told you before that you must brush *gently*?'

'I'm so sorry, Stepsister,' Ash said in a demure voice, and lightened her touch slightly. 'I only thought you must be tired and would wish to go to bed soon.'

'Well,' Ana mused, 'it is true. I am exhausted. I danced nearly all night! Did you know Clara stood at the wall for nearly half the evening? It is a pity she is just not as beautiful as I am.' Ash eyed her stepsister's reflection in the mirror and said nothing.

By the time Ash finished attending both Ana and Clara, who could only talk about how grand the palace was — 'if only you could have seen it, Ash,' she said — it was very late. Gwen had already gone to bed, but she had not yet fallen asleep. As Ash changed into her nightgown, Gwen shifted on the thin mattress and asked, 'Don't you think Colin is handsome?'

Ash slipped beneath the covers and answered, 'I suppose.'

'You suppose?' Gwen cried, and giggled. 'I think he

is wonderful.' She sighed and flung her hands over her head onto the pillow. 'We danced together for three dances tonight,' Gwen said. 'I hope – oh, I shouldn't say anything or I'll invite bad luck.' Gwen turned onto her side, curling her hands beneath her chin, and looked at Ash lying next to her. 'Do you have someone, in West Riding?'

'I – no, I don't,' Ash said. *Not in the way that you mean*, she thought.

'Oh, don't you just yearn for someone?' Gwen said in a breathless voice. 'Someone to take care of you, and hold you, and…' Gwen giggled again, and Ash did not respond. She felt, as always, the loss of her mother, but she knew that was not what Gwen was asking about. 'Oh, I can't wait until I find my husband,' Gwen continued. 'My mother and I have been embroidering linens for my trousseau for ages … what have you been working on?'

'I don't have a trousseau,' Ash said. *Or a mother to help me with one.*

'You don't?' Gwen said, shocked. 'Goodness, you must begin at once. You're so pretty, Ash, you can't expect to be a maid forever. Whom do you wish to marry?'

'I don't know,' Ash said. Gwen's questions made her uncomfortable.

'I mean, do you want him to be tall, dark, fair, a butler, a merchant?' Gwen persisted. 'I think Colin would be ideal for me. We would both be able to stay in the same household.' When Ash didn't respond, Gwen asked, 'Is something wrong?'

'I'm sorry, I suppose I'm just tired,' Ash said.

'All right, all right. Go to sleep then.' But Gwen didn't sound angry with her, just amused, and she turned her back to Ash and fell silent.

Ash lay on her back for some time, staring up at the ceiling, not in the least bit weary. When she heard Gwen's breathing take on the even rhythm of sleep, Ash carefully rolled over onto her side, turning away from Gwen. Her father's second marriage had only made her life miserable, and she had never respected Ana's single-minded quest for a husband. But Gwen's words opened up something inside herself that she had long forgotten: the memory of being loved. Once, things had been different. Tears pricked at her eyes, and she held herself very still, her body tense, not wanting to wake Gwen.

When Ash finally fell asleep, she dreamed of the Wood, the tall dark trees, the shafts of sunlight that shone through the canopy to the soft forest floor. She could smell the spicy pine, the dampness of bark after rain, and the exotic fragrance that clung to Sidhean. It was the scent of jasmine, she remembered, and night-blooming roses that had never felt the touch of a human hand. But though he was walking next to her, she could not turn her head to see him. Instead, she could only look straight ahead, where the huntress was walking purposefully down the path, her green cloak fluttering behind her. If only she would turn around, Ash thought, then the huntress would finally see her. But she would not look back, and Ash could not call out her name, for she did not know it.

When the morning bell tolled and Ash opened her eyes, the dream still clinging to her, she could not at first remember where she was. Then she felt Gwen sit up beside her, and she smelled the cold morning air and heard the creaking of the townhouse as it groaned into life. There were footsteps on the back stairs, and the voice of one of the other maids on the other side of the wall. She was in the City, and Yule was over, and she would be returning to Quinn House that day. Sidhean was waiting.

10

Ash spent the morning packing for their return to
West Riding. She was struggling to fit Ana's newest
acquisition – a heavy velvet wrap lined in rich blue silk
– into her already overstuffed trunk when Gwen
knocked on the open door and came in. She was
carrying a folded piece of paper that she held out to Ash,
who was kneeling on the floor in front of the trunk.

'It's a spell,' Gwen said in a conspiratorial tone.

'What do you mean?' Ash asked, unfolding the paper.
Written in what Ash assumed was Gwen's handwriting
were several lines:

> *Good Lysara, play thy part*
> *Send to me my own sweetheart*
> *Show me such a happy bliss*
> *This night of him to have a kiss.*

'Tomorrow is the Fast of Lysara,' Gwen whispered,
kneeling down next to her and trying ineffectually to

close the trunk.

'Oh,' Ash said. She had first heard the tale of Lysara when she was very young, for it was a popular one, but she hadn't given it a thought in years. Lysara had been a beautiful but penniless young woman from the far Northern Mountains, and when the King, whose name had long been forgotten, first set eyes on her at a Yule bonfire, he fell in love with her, and she with him. The King's advisors disapproved of the match because it was thought that she was half-fairy, for her eyes were as deep and richly verdant as the forest. But even though everyone knew that no good could come of a union with a fairy woman, the King was so deeply in love with her that he arranged to be married within a fortnight. The first year of their marriage was marked by uncommon prosperity and joy, but it was also their last. Exactly one year after their wedding, Lysara died giving birth. During her short reign as Queen, the people had grown to love her dearly, for she was the embodiment of true love, steadfast and sweet. So the anniversary of her wedding day became known as the Fast of Lysara, when young girls made wishes upon their clean linen pillows to dream of their true love.

'Lysara watches over us,' Gwen insisted, giving up on latching the trunk shut. 'You must fast tomorrow in her honour, and before you go to sleep, say this spell – my mother's aunt gave it to me, and she knows a greenwitch who says it will work – and you'll dream of your future husband. That way you'll recognize him when you see him.'

Ash must have looked startled, and Gwen misread her expression as apprehension. 'It's all right,' Gwen said reassuringly. 'We all do it – all of us servants, anyway. We just don't tell the mistress. And it won't hurt to give it a try.'

'Thank you,' Ash said, bemused, and slipped the note into her pocket. 'I'll try.'

'Good,' Gwen said. She impulsively reached out and pulled Ash into an embrace. 'It's been good to have you here, Ash. I hope you'll come back with Ana again.'

Ash awkwardly put her arms around Gwen. 'I'll try,' she said again.

Quinn House was cold and dark when they returned later that afternoon. While Jonas carried the trunks back upstairs, Ash lit the fires and began to prepare supper. She was surprised to find that she missed the bustle and excitement of the Page Street mansion; she missed being one of many, easily overlooked. She thought about Gwen, who wanted so desperately to dream of Colin; she thought about Ana, who wanted a life of luxury. What did she want for herself? Ash swept a pile of dried peas into the kettle hanging over the kitchen fire and added a handful of ham. She stoked the fire, and as the flames leapt up she remembered the bonfire, and the dancers, and the look on the huntress's face. Ash put the lid on the kettle and did not think about her question any more.

★ ★ ★

The next morning, Ana did not come downstairs for breakfast. Lady Isobel sipped at her tea and said, 'Aisling, go upstairs and see what is taking Ana so long. Her breakfast is getting cold.'

When Ash opened the door to Ana's room, she found her stepsister awake and sitting at the window looking out at the courtyard, dusted with snow. 'Your mother is asking for you,' Ash said.

'I'm not going down,' Ana replied. 'Tell her I'm ill today.'

Ash eyed her stepsister skeptically. She did not seem ill. In fact, Ana was particularly lively, with a glow in her cheeks and a sparkle in her eyes that made her look as if she were holding back a secret. 'You don't look unwell,' Ash observed.

Ana's brow creased in annoyance. 'Tell her I'm sick,' she stated again. 'And don't bring me any food; I can't stand it right now.'

Ash shrugged and went to deliver the message, but her stepmother insisted that she bring Ana a boiled egg and some tea. When she carried the tray upstairs, she found Ana sitting in the same position. 'Your mother told me to bring this for you,' Ash said, depositing the tray on the small table by the window seat.

'Take it away; I won't eat it,' Ana said.

'Fine,' Ash said curtly. 'I'll just tell your mother you wouldn't eat. She'll probably call the physician.'

This caused Ana to actually look worried for a moment, and then she turned to Ash and said, 'Aisling, I really can't eat it, but you mustn't tell Mother.'

Ash looked at her stepsister's face, flushed with desperation and hope, and said, 'You're fasting, aren't you?'

Ana coloured, asking unconvincingly, 'Why would I do that?'

Ash shook her head. 'I wouldn't have thought you had it in you,' she said archly, 'to revert to old superstitions.'

'I don't know what you're talking about,' Ana said, and turned away from Ash.

But Ash could still see her stepsister's cheeks, pink from the lie. She reached into her pocket and pulled out the folded note that Gwen had given her. Walking over to her stepsister, she placed the paper on the window seat. 'Here,' she said. 'Read this aloud before you go to bed tonight.' She picked up the untouched tray and began to leave the room.

'You won't tell Mother?' Ana said in a low voice.

'I won't,' Ash promised. She took the tray back down to the kitchen, where she poured herself a cup of tea from Ana's untouched pot, and very deliberately cracked the egg on the countertop, watching the shell splinter. She peeled it away and salted the damp, slippery white surface of the egg. When she bit off the top, the yolk fell in golden crumbles onto the scarred wooden table.

* * *

That night, after the supper dishes were washed and put away and her stepmother and stepsisters had retired to their beds, Ash sat wrapped in a warm quilt on the hearth, nodding over a book of hunting stories she had found in the library. She was half-dreaming about horses and hounds and a leaping white stag when the last log on the fire cracked, sending cinders crashing through the grate. She awoke with a start and then decided to drag herself off to bed.

As she lay her head down on the pillow she could feel herself falling into a dream, as if she were tumbling into a well involuntarily, and when she stopped falling she found herself walking down a path through the Wood. She recognized it almost immediately: This was the path that led to Rook Hill. She could see the ground ahead of her, illuminated, and she realized she was carrying a lantern in her right hand and a spade in her left. She had not been walking for long before she saw her destination: the hawthorn tree and her mother's grave. But unlike in previous dreams, this time she had no trouble reaching the end of the path. When she emerged from the Wood, she looked towards the grave and knew with a sense of rising dread that something was wrong. She took the last few steps, her legs shaking, and saw that there was a gaping hole where there should have been earth and grass.

She shone the lantern light into the open grave,

and the roots of the hawthorn tree jutted out from the soil like gnarled fingers, reaching for something that had been snatched away. The light fell on the spade she held, and she saw dirt on the blade, and the torn end of a tree root.

Her heart was pounding in her chest, and she awoke abruptly, her breath rasping in her lungs. The moonlight was streaming in through the cracks in the shutters, and she felt herself damp with sweat. The hall clock began chiming, and she counted twelve strokes before it fell silent. She lay down again and tried to go back to sleep, but the memory of the dream was too strong. Finally, she threw off the blankets and dressed in her warmest leggings and a thick woollen dress, and then opened the small trunk at the foot of her bed and pulled out the silvery cloak. She swirled it over her shoulders and went out the kitchen door.

The moon was full that night, casting a clear white light over the field and the line of the Wood in the distance. She left the kitchen garden behind her, closed the gate with a soft click, and set off across the field. The night air was like a whip against her skin, and she pulled the hood of the cloak over her head and hunched her shoulders against the cold. She felt anxious and twitchy, and as she walked all the events of the past week flooded through her mind: dressing Ana for the masque; the rain of gold coins at the bonfire; the words of Gwen's girlish spell. And beneath it all, the dream of the empty grave making her stomach turn.

She paused for a moment at the edge of the Wood and looked back across the field at the bulk of the house, dark and still. She thrust her hands into the cloak's interior pockets, and it rippled like the trail of a quick fish through a silent pond. Then she raised her head to the dark Wood and looked for what she was seeking. At first she only saw the trees: tall trunks edged with moonlight, fading into black-upon-black in the distance. As her eyes adjusted to the night, she gradually began to pick out the shapes along the ground, and finally she saw it: the slight signs of the beginnings of a trail. She turned towards the path and began walking.

The Wood was dark and silent, the moonlight threading its way down between naked branches to shed long dark shadows along the ground. Soon the thin, overgrown trail became a path, and then the path opened into a lane wide enough for two horses to walk abreast. She had been walking for just over an hour when she heard the music in the distance: pipes and lutes and high, clear voices singing. The music was so beautiful she ached to run to it, but she kept her feet on the path and her eyes focused forward. She pulled the cloak closer around her as if it were armour, and tried not to listen to the music. There was laughter, too, the bright sparkling laughter of women and the answering tones of men in a language she could not understand,

and it made her quiver with the urge to find the people who spoke those words.

She began to run then, forcing herself onwards even though fear pulsed inside her. When she recognized the gentle slope that descended past the last few trees into the clearing behind the old house at Rook Hill, she almost sobbed with relief. She broke free of the great heavy arms of the Wood and emerged, breathless, at the hawthorn tree. She knelt down beside her mother's grave, which was whole and untouched, and wiped away the dirt and moss that had overgrown the headstone. She lay her head down upon it and closed her eyes.

Almost immediately she felt the warmth of her mother's embrace, her hands smoothing back the hood of the fairy cloak and brushing her dark hair away from her face. *Mother,* she tried to ask. *What must I do? I cannot go on the way I have been . . .*

Her mother answered, *There will come a change, and you will know what to do.*

But when Ash tried to demand a more specific answer, she felt her mother slip away from her as if she were made of melting snow, and when she held her tighter, there was only the tombstone beneath her hands. She felt a gaping emptiness within her that hurt like nothing she had ever felt before, as if this time, finally, was the last time her mother would come to her. From the depths of that emptiness came an upwelling of rage that made her push herself away from the grave.

'How could you leave me?' she cried out loud, scrambling up on to her feet. Her voice sounded ugly and guttural to her ears, and she did not feel like herself. She wanted to kick the gravestone; she wanted to tear out the earth beneath which her mother lay and pull the body out of the ground and shake it until it gave her an answer. She fell to the ground again and dug her fingers into the winter-hard earth, scrabbling at the soil until her fingers began to bleed.

The ground would not come up. It was frozen. Her mother was dead.

Numbed with cold, feeling as though the inside of herself had been scraped raw, Ash stood up on shaky legs several minutes later and turned her back on the grave to go back into the Wood. This time when she heard the music, she went towards it. Leaving the path, she picked her way across fallen branches and drifts of snow, and soon she saw flickering lights like fireflies in midsummer. The trees parted to reveal a mossy clearing hung with strings of silver lanterns, and in the centre of the clearing a bonfire was lit, sparking and burning with unnaturally red flames. Around the fire a circle of girls danced, and some of the girls were human like herself, except when she looked at their faces, they looked mad.

Some people said that girls who were tempted to enter fairy rings lost all of their humanity from the ecstasy of the dancing. Others said that only a girl who was mad would enter a fairy ring in the first place. Ash decided that perhaps she was mad that night, so she stepped past the lanterns and entered the clearing. All around the dancing circle, men and women – no, these were fairies in their unearthly splendour – lay on cushions, crystal goblets in hand. When she entered the circle they looked at her and smiled, and then someone next to her fingered the cloak she was wearing and spoke to another in a musical language she didn't understand. One of the fairy women approached her, her skin nearly translucent it was so pale, her eyes hard like sapphires, but the smile on her face was entrancing.

In a lilting voice she asked, 'Why are you so sad, little girl? We are all joy here.'

Ash couldn't answer, because her grief and anger now seemed so superfluous in comparison to the perfection of this fairy woman, who took her hand to lead her into the dancing circle. The woman's hand was strong and supple, and Ash saw that despite the fact that it was winter, she wore only a thin dress made of what looked like cobwebs, or maybe moonlight, if it could be run through a fairy loom. Then Ash felt someone take her other hand and pull her back away from the dancing girls, and the fairy woman turned to look at who had restrained her. The sharp anger in the woman's eyes startled her; it was as if a beautiful mask had slid off to reveal the hungry beast within. Ash recoiled from her and looked back at the person who was pulling her away, and it was Sidhean.

He was furious; she could see the muscles of his face taut beneath his white skin, and he roared at the fairy woman in their foreign tongue. Ash felt the woman let go of her, and Sidhean dragged her out of the circle, his fingers nearly crushing her arm. 'You're hurting me,' she gasped, but he would not stop moving until they were well removed from that place and she could no longer hear the intoxicating music.

'What were you doing?' he demanded at last, letting go of her as though she burned him.

'I had a dream,' she said, and she felt confused, lightheaded; the glamour of the circle still clung to her and she looked around desperately, trying to find any trace of it in the distance.

'A dream,' he repeated coldly. 'A dream of what?'

'I dreamed of my mother's grave,' she said, and as she spoke it seemed to help banish the magic a little. She began to feel the heft of the cloak around her shoulders and the night air on her skin. 'I dreamed,' she said, 'that it was empty – that she had been taken.'

She looked up at him with unfocussed eyes; there was some kind of fog between the two of them. He grasped her shoulders and shook her. 'Your mother is dead,' he said forcefully.

She twisted out of his hands. 'Stop it – don't say that!' she shouted at him, angry.

Perhaps her vehemence cleared away the last of the glamour, because Ash suddenly saw him staring intently at her, and for the first time the skin and bones of his face were knitted together into one, and he looked – to her astonishment – like he was worried. Something inside her crumpled; a weight settled. 'I know she is dead,' she said, and at last, it felt like something that had happened long ago.

She took his hands in hers, and for the first time she felt him warm at her touch. She had seen the wild, ancient creature in him before, but this time that inhumanness edged into something she recognized with her gut: He looked at her with desire. It was overwhelming in its intensity, and she felt as though she could not breathe.

He spoke as if he could not help himself: 'You look like her.' And he cupped her head in his hands, turning her up to face the moonlight sliding through the tree branches.

His words registered dimly at first, for she was mostly aware of him, his nearness, but as the silence filled the space between them she realized what he had said. She closed her eyes, feeling his thumbs trace the line of her lips. She asked in a faint voice, 'Who do I look like?'

He pulled away from her slowly, as if reluctant to let her go, and when she opened her eyes he had turned away. Finally he said, 'Elinor. You look like Elinor.'

The name hung between them like a ghost.

Astonished, Ash said, 'Do you mean my mother?' He nodded very slightly, but still would not face her. She went to him and put her hand on his arm and asked, 'What was she like?'

He made a sound that she recognized as something of a laugh. 'She was … she was different from any other human woman I have known,' he said. 'She was not afraid. She was stronger than I expected.'

'What do you mean?' Ash asked. 'What did you expect?'

'Humans are weak,' he answered. 'They are easily tempted. But not … not Elinor.'

She asked, 'Am I like her?'

He turned to her and swept a strand of hair out of her eyes, his fingers leaving a burning trail on her skin. 'In some ways you are,' he said. 'But you are more reckless than she ever was.'

'How am I reckless?'

'Every time you come near me,' he said, 'you come closer to the end of everything.'

'It does not feel that way,' she said. 'It feels like I am coming closer to the beginning.'

'You do not understand.'

'Then explain it to me,' she said, and took his hands in hers. His fingers were curled up into fists, hard and closed.

'It is not time,' he said, and she felt him withdrawing from her.

She held his fists more tightly in her hands and asked, 'What did you tell that – that woman?'

'I told her that you were mine; that I had given you this cloak; that she could not have you.' The tone of his voice was curiously flat, as if he were reining himself in. He turned away from her and said, 'I will take you home.'

They stood in silence until the white horse emerged, ghostly pale, out of the dark. He mounted the horse and then reached down to help her up behind him. 'Hold on,' he told her, and turned the horse away from the fairy ring. She slid her arms around his waist, twisting to see if she could catch a last glimpse of the dancing circle, but there was nothing there.

The rhythm of the horse's paces lulled Ash into sleepiness, and she lay her head upon his back, closing her eyes for what she thought was only a moment. When Sidhean pulled the horse to a halt, she awoke and saw that they had reached the edge of the Wood. 'You will walk from here,' Sidhean said to her. 'It is almost dawn.'

She slid off the horse and it was a long way down, and when she looked up at him, he seemed very tall and strange. 'Thank you,' she said.

He nodded, and then took something out of a pocket and handed it down to her. It was a round silver medallion with a jewel in the centre, and in the depths of it a faint light glimmered. Around the rim strange words were written, and though she could not read them, their shapes were beautiful, as light as flying birds. 'Take this,' he told her, 'and if you should need something . . . impossible . . . use it to find me.'

She held it in her hands and asked, 'Why are you giving this to me? Why have you never killed me? In all the tales, no human—'

'Your tales do not tell the whole story,' he interrupted her. He looked down at her for a moment, the light of dawn seeking out the colour of his eyes and making him look almost human. Then he turned his horse around to go back into the Wood, and she watched him go, feeling as if her world had split wide open. On the other side it was not dark as midnight, but rather bright as sunshine in the middle of winter: blinding, dazzling on the snow.

Part Two

The Huntress

11

Ana was already awake when Ash came in to light the fire the next morning; she was sitting in the chair by her window overlooking the front yard. 'Good morning,' Ash said, and as she knelt on the cold hearth she felt the weight of the medallion in her pocket, banging gently against her thigh.

'Good morning,' Ana said.

'Did you sleep well?' Ash asked.

'Does it matter?' Ana replied.

Ash looked over her shoulder at her stepsister; she was staring out the window with a bitter expression on her face. Ash shrugged. 'I was merely asking.'

'I'm fine,' Ana snapped.

Ash stood up when the fire was lit and turned to face her stepsister. 'I gather that you did not dream of who you wished?' she said.

Ana glared at her. 'If you are insinuating that I used that ridiculous poem you gave me yesterday to divine for my future husband, you are sorely mistaken. I was simply feeling unwell. Today I am much better and would like you to bring me my breakfast.'

Ash looked at her stepsister steadily and said, 'It's not surprising it didn't work – you can't see what you don't believe in.'

'Get out of my room,' Ana said in a cold voice. 'I'm not interested in your rustic explanations.'

Ash couldn't help it – she laughed at her. When Ana shot her a furious look, Ash put a hand over her mouth and mumbled, 'I'm sorry—'

Ana stood up, fists clenched. 'Yes, "rustic,"' she said angrily. 'What do you know of anything but the country? Isn't that where those stupid fairy stories come from? I know you still read them – crouching all covered in soot on the hearth because you're too *rustic* to know how to sit in the parlour. You must still believe that they are real and not merely tall tales for children.'

Ash opened her mouth but did not know what to say. She could show her stepsister the medallion in her pocket, but Ana would only think she had stolen it. Her stepsister continued, 'You traipse around the house thinking you're too good for us – I know you do. I've seen the way you look at us, the way you look at *me*. You think I'm a spoiled little brat only looking for a rich man to buy me jewels, but you don't know *anything*, Aisling. How else are we going to live? How else is my mother ever going to pay off her debts unless I marry well? If your father hadn't left so many debts, we wouldn't have to live like this, with you waiting on us with your clumsy hands and ugly manners.'

Ash snapped, 'If your mother stopped spending all her money on furs and jewels and new gowns, perhaps you wouldn't be so desperate for a rich husband.'

Ana lunged at her and slapped her across the face. Ash recoiled in shock, her hand covering her pink cheek. 'How dare you insult my mother,' said Ana. 'You are nothing more than a low country girl who believes in archaic superstitions. You'll never become more than that, Aisling. Never. Now get out of my room.'

Furious, Ash turned and stalked out of her stepsister's room. Ana slammed the door behind her, and the force of it shook the house.

For the rest of that week, Ana took it upon herself to be particularly unpleasant to her. Ash went about her work in silence as Ana upbraided her about her poor cooking skills, the invisible layer of dust on the dining room table, the unevenness of her stitching on their stockings. The constant criticism grated on her nerves, and as soon as she could escape – on an afternoon when Ana and Clara and Lady Isobel went into the City – she fled the house.

She was halfway across the meadow, stomping down the grasses in frustration, when she saw the buck standing at the edge of the trees. He seemed to look at Ash for a long moment, his ears perked forward, and then turned to go back into the Wood. Without thinking, Ash went after him, pulling her cloak more securely around herself. It calmed her to follow him, his delicate hoofprints marking a way out of the maze of her thoughts. By the time she lost the trail it was midmorning, and she had gone farther than she expected. She thought that she was likely near the edge of the King's Forest, where it blurred into the greater Wood. She closed her eyes for a moment and breathed in the smell of the forest, and perhaps because her eyes were closed, she heard the approaching footsteps more clearly. It was from a very light tread – this person knew how to move quietly in a forest full of fallen twigs and leaves – and when the sound stopped, Ash knew the person had seen her.

She opened her eyes and looked at the King's Huntress, who was standing where Ash had come from. 'You were following the buck,' the woman said.

'I lost him,' Ash said.

The huntress looked past her and raised an arm to point at a spot in the distance. 'He's gone that way.'

'How do you know?'

The huntress walked in the direction that she had pointed and gestured for Ash to follow her. She squatted down next to a sapling and said, 'You see here: how this leaf is broken, and if you look carefully, you can see the smudge of a hoofprint.'

Ash stared down at the ground and perhaps, yes,

there was a broken leaf, but the hoofprint was so faint that it was hardly visible. 'How could you see that?' she asked.

The woman grinned. 'I know where he's going. He beds down for the day in a grove just up there.' She tapped her hand on the sapling and said, 'You did a good job, though, tracking him this far. It was a difficult trail to follow.'

'Thank you,' Ash said.

The huntress looked at her curiously and asked, 'Who taught you to track?'

'No one,' Ash answered. 'I don't know how.'

'Then how did you follow the buck?'

She said simply, 'I looked for him.'

'Well,' said the woman, 'you have sharp eyes.'

'I've seen you before,' Ash said impulsively, and blushed.

'And where was that?' the woman asked, amused.

Ash hesitated. 'At . . . at Yule, of course.'

'In the City?' the huntress said.

'Yes.'

'But you do not live in the City, do you? What are you doing wandering around the Wood?'

'I . . . like the Wood,' Ash said.

The woman reached out and fingered the material of the cloak Ash was wearing. 'And wearing a king's ransom on your back as well,' she observed.

Suddenly self-conscious, Ash pulled the cloak more

tightly around herself. 'I didn't steal it,' she said sharply.

The huntress frowned. 'I didn't say you did.'
There was an awkward silence between them, and
Ash looked down at the ground, studying the gradations
of brown and the pattern of veins in the fallen leaves.
Eventually the huntress said, 'All right then, well, have
a good walk,' and turned to go back the way she
had come.

But Ash reached out and grabbed her arm and asked,
'Please, will you show me the way back to the path? I
think I'm lost.'

The woman looked down at Ash's hand on her and
Ash quickly withdrew it, but the woman merely nodded
and said, 'This way.'

They walked through the Wood without speaking,
but their steps seemed as loud as an advancing army.
Walking behind the huntress, Ash watched the rise and
fall of her shoulders as she moved, her green woollen
cloak flapping behind her with each sure-footed step.
When they reached the trail, the huntress paused and
asked, 'Where are you going?'

'To West Riding,' Ash responded. 'I think I know
where I am now, thank you.'

The huntress said, 'Then I'll bid you good morning.'
She extended her gloved hand, and Ash reached out
with her bare one and they clasped fingers firmly, and
the huntress looked a bit confused. Then she said, 'I've
seen you before as well.'

'You have?'

'Yes,' she said. 'Last fall, on the riverbank. Wasn't that you?'

Ash remembered the light on the water that day, the way the sun sparkled off the droplets falling from the huntress's fingers. 'Yes,' she said, 'that was me.'

The huntress laughed suddenly. 'Then we are old friends, aren't we?'

'I don't know your name,' said Ash.

'I'm Kaisa.'

'I'm Ash.'

A bugle sounded in the distance, and Kaisa said, 'I'm called.'

'Do you hunt today?' Ash asked.

'No – we're heading back to the City this morning, actually.' She sounded regretful. 'And the deer are not in season yet.'

'Why are you here today, then?'

Kaisa looked surprised, but answered, 'I cannot go too long without this forest.'

'Nor can I,' Ash agreed, and they shared a smile.

The huntress nodded to her and said, 'I must go. Good day to you.'

'Good day,' Ash replied, and then, because it did not seem polite to watch her walking away, Ash turned down the path toward West Riding. As she walked, she touched the trees one by one as if she were marking the path, as if her handprints left glowing traces on the bark.

She felt a little guilty because she had lied to the huntress, and she wondered if the huntress had known, for Ash had not been lost that day.

Ana returned from the City that evening with a gleam in her eye; she even seemed to forget that she was angry with Ash. That night while Ash was helping Clara undress for bed, she asked what had put her in such a good mood, and Clara said, 'Ana believes she has found her husband.'

'Really?' Ash said, surprised. 'So soon?'

Clara smiled slightly. 'Lord Rowan is his name. They met at Yule, but today he paid her a great attention.'

'What is he like?' Ash asked.

Clara shrugged. 'He is wealthy,' she said, and would say no more.

Later that week a letter arrived for Ana, and Ash saw her stepsister's face light up with excitement as she handed it to her.

'It *is* from Lord Rowan,' Ana said, examining the seal. She tore it open eagerly, running her eyes down the page.

'Well, what does it say?' Lady Isobel demanded impatiently.

Ana looked smug as she reported, 'He has invited me – and you, of course, Mother, and Clara as well – to visit him at his country house in Royal Forge. For an entire week!'

'That's wonderful,' Clara said, though Ash somehow doubted her sincerity.

But Lady Isobel was beaming. 'He is a very generous man,' she said proudly. And then she glanced at Ash and said curtly, 'Go and fetch us some writing materials. We must respond immediately.'

A week later, Ana, Clara, and Lady Isobel drove off to spend a week at Royal Forge. Ash was left behind, for Lord Rowan had assured Ana that she would want for nothing during her visit. Lady Isobel, who viewed it as a punishment for Ash, did not object.

12

The evening after her stepmother and stepsisters left, Ash wandered through the Wood until she came to a massive, low-hanging oak limb. She settled down on the mossy surface, and as dusk fell she saw a doe and two fawns emerge from the underbrush on legs as slender as reeds. The two fawns were still young enough to have speckled coats, but as the summer went on they would lose their spots and become as brown as their mother. They were browsing slowly down the path to the river, but then the mother stopped and raised her head, her large ears perking in two different directions. She swung her head around and looked straight at Ash, her eyes huge and glimmering, and then she took off, leaping away. The fawns followed suit, their hooves crushing the dried leaves as they bounded through the Wood.

Ash shifted on the branch, feeling the tree move beneath her, and she wondered if she would see Sidhean that night. She took the medallion out of her pocket and cupped it in her hands, looking at it, but the stone was opaque and revealed nothing. It was as beautiful and inscrutable, she thought, as he was. Then she saw movement out of the corner of her eye and she looked up, hopeful, but it was not him. Instead, she saw Kaisa coming down the path slowly, as if she were looking for something. At the fork in the path she dropped down to examine the ground, and Ash realized that she was following the trail of the deer.

Ash said, 'They went down to the river.'

Startled, Kaisa stood up swiftly and looked for the source of the words. 'Where are you?' she asked.

Ash climbed down off the branch, and the movement in the dim light caught the huntress's eye. 'Here,' Ash said. She came onto the path, and it took a moment for the huntress to recognize her, for most of the daylight was gone.

'Oh,' said Kaisa in surprise.

'I'm sorry if I startled you,' Ash said.

Kaisa shook her head. 'It's all right.' She paused and then said, 'You must live nearby.'

'Yes,' said Ash. 'The house on the far side of the meadow.'

They stood in silence for a few moments, separated by a body's length of the deepening darkness, and Ash suddenly felt self-conscious, not knowing what to say. But then there were footsteps coming down the path towards them, and another woman appeared, carrying an armful of kindling. She was dressed like Kaisa, in

148

riding clothes, but in the low light, Ash could not see her face. 'There you are,' the woman began, and then saw Ash. 'I thought you were going to gather some wood,' she said to Kaisa.

Kaisa turned to her and answered, 'I was.' She looked back at Ash and asked, 'Can you find your way home?'

'Yes,' Ash said, and then Kaisa went to the woman, taking some of the kindling from her. Ash stepped back off the trail, looking down, as the two women passed her, taking care to pull her cloak out of the way. As they moved out of sight, Ash heard the woman ask who she was, but she could not hear Kaisa's reply.

She waited until the moon rose before she went home, but though she looked carefully around her, she met no one on her walk back to Quinn House. The disappointment inside her was thick and heavy.

She was in the garden the next day, weeding, when she saw the rider out in the meadow. She straightened up, shading her eyes from the noonday sun with one dirt-smeared hand, and slowly the rider came into focus: a green cloak, a bay horse, a shock of dark hair. It was the King's Huntress, and when she reached the iron gate she called out, 'Good afternoon!'

'Good afternoon,' Ash replied, surprised, and before she could think, she asked, 'What are you doing here?'

The huntress laughed. 'I am sorry – I did not mean to interrupt you. I was just out for a ride and I admit I was curious about whether this was the house you spoke of last night.'

'Oh,' Ash said, and then stammered, 'it — it is, yes. This is where I live.'

Kaisa dismounted from her horse and asked, 'May I ask you for some water for my horse?'

'Of course,' Ash said, and brushed the dirt off her hands onto her apron. 'Please, wait just a moment — I'll be right back.' She went inside the kitchen for the water bucket, and then came back outside to the pump.

'Thank you,' said the huntress.

The cool water splashed over the edge of the bucket as Ash lifted it. 'It's nothing,' she said, and carried it to the back gate. The huntress undid the latch and pulled the gate open for her, and then Ash set the bucket down on the ground for the bay mare.

Kaisa gestured to the garden and asked, 'Are you the gardener?'

'In a way,' Ash answered, feeling uncomfortable. 'I — I am the housekeeper, of sorts.'

'I see,' said Kaisa, and smiled at her. Ash felt slightly flustered.

'Are you — are you hunting today?' she asked, trying to make conversation.

Kaisa shook her head. 'No. It is too early in the season.'

'Of course,' Ash said, and was embarrassed.

The huntress gave her a rueful smile and asked,

'Would you mind if I came inside and drank some of your water as well? I admit I did not bring any with me, and it has been a long ride already – I am not sure why I was so forgetful today.'

'Of course,' Ash said again, surprised by the request. 'Will your horse need to be tied up?'

Kaisa shook her head, taking off her riding gloves. 'No, no, she'll be fine here.'

Ash led the huntress up the garden path and into the kitchen, and she poured some water from the pitcher on the scarred kitchen table into a clean goblet. When she handed it to her, she took care not to touch Kaisa's hand with her own dirtied one. She watched the huntress's throat as she swallowed, and she wondered if Kaisa could hear the pounding of her heart. She was nervous, afraid that she would do something wrong; would the huntress report it to Lady Isobel? She turned away and went to the sink, plunging her hands into the dishpan and trying to scrub off some of the soil that had lodged beneath her nails.

'This is a pleasant kitchen,' said Kaisa.

'Thank you,' Ash said, continuing to wash her hands. Her mind raced: What did one do when the King's Huntress stopped by unexpectedly? Should she offer her something? 'Would you like anything to eat?' she asked, and then she wondered for a panicked moment if she even had any food to offer her.

'I don't want to trouble you,' Kaisa said.

'It's no trouble,' Ash said, and turned to look for a kitchen towel, only to find the huntress holding one out for her, a slight smile on her face.

'Then I would be happy to eat,' Kaisa said, and Ash blushed, taking the towel.

She found a loaf of bread that was only a day old, and a wedge of cheese that she had been saving for her own dinner, and a couple of apples – the last ones from the previous year. As she sliced into the bread, the huntress set her gloves down on the table, then sat down on one of the benches. She picked up the book that was lying open near a candle stub and asked, 'What are you reading?'

'Just an old book,' Ash said, trying to keep her tone light. She didn't understand what interest the King's Huntress had in this household – or in her.

Kaisa turned the pages of the book curiously. 'Fairy tales,' she observed.

'It is a book I had as a child,' Ash said.

Kaisa looked up at her. 'Do you have a favourite tale?' she asked.

Ash shrugged, and put the bread on a plate alongside the cheese. She began to peel an apple. 'I'm not sure,' she hedged.

'I have a favourite,' Kaisa said, and she did not seem to think it was anything to be embarrassed about. 'Do you wish to hear it?' Once again Ash was surprised, and the paring knife slipped and nicked her finger, leaving behind a thin line of blood. 'Be careful,' said Kaisa, and reached out to take the knife away from her. Ash relinquished it, raising her finger to her mouth, and the huntress slid the blade under the rosy skin of the apple, peeling it off in a single smooth strip.

'I think of it as more of a hunting story than a fairy tale,' Kaisa said, 'though there are fairies in it. Another huntress told it to me, when I was a little girl.' Ash sat down across from her and put the bread and cheese between them, and the huntress began to slice the apple as she spoke.

'It is about one of the earliest huntresses in the kingdom, Niamh, who was the daughter of a powerful greenwitch. When the King chose Niamh as his huntress, he asked her to teach his daughter, Rois, to hunt, for he valued Niamh's knowledge and wanted Rois to know his lands as well as Niamh did. Rois was a beautiful young woman, sweet and strong, and Niamh was impressed with her abilities. As they rode together week after week, month after month, Niamh found that she was falling in love with Rois, and her heart ached, for Rois was promised to the prince of a neighbouring kingdom, and she loved him, it is said, with a purity of heart that Niamh could not change.'

'So Niamh went to her mother, the powerful greenwitch, and begged for a potion that would change Rois's heart. But her mother knew that such a potion would be a dark magic, and though she wanted her daughter to be happy, she told her, "If you wish the impossible, you must be willing to give up everything you hold dear." She told Niamh that the only way Rois could be made to love her was if Niamh sought out the Fairy Queen and asked her to grant this wish.'

'Because she yearned for Rois to love her, Niamh saw no other choice. She bid farewell to the King and to Rois, and rode off in search of the road to Taninli, the city of the Fairy Queen. She rode for many days through the deepest parts of the Wood, and at last, driven by her desire to claim Rois's heart, she found the crystal gates leading to Taninli. When she rode through the gates all the fairies looked at her in wonder, for few humans had ever walked their streets.'

'When Niamh came to the Fairy Queen's palace, she presented herself at the great diamond doors and asked for admission, and the doors opened. The Fairy Queen, they say, was more beautiful than any creature in the land, and every human who saw her would fall in love with her upon first sight. When Niamh saw her, she did indeed think her very beautiful, but she remembered why she had come, and she asked for her wish. The Queen, who admired Niamh's courage in coming to seek her out, agreed to grant her wish on one condition: If Niamh remained in Taninli for ten years and acted as the Queen's own huntress, then at the end of that time she could return to the human world, and Rois would love her as she had loved no man before.'

'So Niamh, of course, accepted the condition. Ten years was nothing compared to a lifetime, she thought. But she had not counted on the effect the Fairy Queen would have on her, and as the years passed, she discovered that she loved Rois less and less, and the Fairy Queen more and more. The Queen herself found, to her surprise, that her admiration for Niamh was turning into love. So at the end of the ten years, she asked Niamh if she truly wanted her wish to be granted, and Niamh wept openly and said that she loved the Queen and no longer wished for Rois's heart to change. And the Queen took her in her arms and kissed her, and Niamh spent the rest of her days in Taninli, happily at the side of the Fairy Queen.'

When Kaisa finished the story, the food lay untouched between them, but the apple had been sliced neatly into six wedges, the skin coiled like a ribbon around them. 'Please,' said the huntress, 'will you eat?'

Ash picked up a piece of the apple and bit into it, and the flesh was crisp and sweet.

Afterwards, as they walked back through the garden to Kaisa's horse, the huntress said, 'Thank you for the water and the food.'

'You are welcome,' Ash replied, and opened the gate for her. Kaisa's elbow brushed against Ash's arm as she passed through the gate. As she mounted her horse, Ash looked up at her and said, 'I do have a favourite fairy tale.'

'You do?'

'Yes. Perhaps one day I will tell it to you,' Ash said.

The huntress looked down at her with a grin and said, 'I hope that you will.' Ash felt herself smiling as well. Then the huntress turned her horse towards the Wood and left Ash with her hand on the gate, watching as the horse and rider were swallowed by the trees in the distance.

13

The huntress's horse was tethered at the edge of the village green on the next market day, but though Ash swept her eyes around the green, she did not see Kaisa herself. Impulsively, she went to the horse and held her hand out; the mare sniffed at her empty palm and then looked at her with gleaming brown eyes that seemed to reproach her for not having an apple to share. Ash laughed out loud and stroked the horse's neck; her black mane was soft as silk.

'Have you ever ridden a hunting horse?' said a voice behind her, and Ash turned to see the huntress walking towards them.

Ash felt herself tense up nervously, and she answered, 'No, I haven't.'

'Would you like to?' Kaisa asked, swinging a saddlebag off her shoulder and buckling it onto the back of her horse's saddle.

'Oh, yes,' Ash said eagerly, and then it occurred to her that the huntress might have been making her an offer, and perhaps she – a common household servant – should have turned her down.

But the huntress said, as if it were the most ordinary thing in the world, 'Then I'll come tomorrow?'

For a moment, Ash was not sure if she had heard her correctly. She stared at Kaisa, who finished tightening the straps of the saddlebags before looking back at her. She was slightly taller than Ash, and she rested her left arm on the horse's withers; the sleeves of her tunic were pushed up, and her hands were bare. She seemed to expect her to say yes. Ash opened her mouth to do so, but then remembered that her stepmother would be at home. 'I cannot, not tomorrow,' Ash said, her heart sinking as she realized that she really did wish to say yes.

Kaisa seemed unperturbed and merely asked, 'When will you be free?'

She stepped back so that she would not be in the way as the huntress came around to unhitch her horse. 'I – I suppose I could go the day after tomorrow,' she said, feeling awkward. Her stepmother and stepsisters would be in the City then.

'Then I will bring a second horse on the day after tomorrow,' Kaisa said, and smiled at her.

Though Ash looked out the kitchen window every few minutes on the morning Kaisa said she would come, part of her did not believe it would actually happen. So when she saw the huntress outside the garden gate with a black horse in tow, she had to look twice to make sure she was not imagining it. She went outside to greet her, but before she could say anything Kaisa asked, 'Do you have riding clothes?'

'No.'

'Then you should wear these.' The huntress handed her a cloth bag cinched shut with a leather tie. When Ash hesitated, Kaisa said, 'Go on – I'll wait for you.' So Ash went back inside and changed into the dark brown leggings and long-sleeved green tunic. They fitted almost as if they had been made for her, but for a tiny scar in the knee where the breeches had been mended. They were more comfortable than the borrowed livery she had worn at Yule. These were made for a woman, and Ash wondered whose clothes they were and how Kaisa had known they would fit her. The thought disconcerted her, and she hurriedly laced up her well-worn boots. Then, taking a deep breath, she went back outside. The huntress stood with her back to the house, gazing out at the meadow. She turned when she heard Ash coming. 'Those seem to fit,' she said, and opened the gate for Ash.

'Thank you for bringing them,' Ash said, wondering if her face were as flushed as she felt.

'You can't ride a hunting horse in a dress,' Kaisa said with a grin, and Ash laughed apprehensively.

'I don't know if I can ride a hunting horse at all,' she said.

'There is no need to worry. Jewel is an experienced teacher,' Kaisa said, stroking the black mare's neck. Ash looked at Jewel dubiously – she might be an experienced horse, but to Ash's eye, Jewel was grander than any horse she had ever ridden. Except, she realized, the times she had ridden with Sidhean. The thought of him in the mid-morning light, with the huntress standing before her, was jarring.

Kaisa saw the changed expression on her face and she took it for nervousness. 'Truly,' she said gently, 'I won't let any harm come to you.'

Her words brought Ash back to that moment, standing at the edge of the meadow in the sunlight with two beautiful hunting horses before her, their coats glossy and smooth – for of course they were the King's horses and must have a stable full of grooms to attend them. And the King's Huntress was there, too, looking at her with concern, and Ash suddenly laughed out loud.

'I apologize,' Ash said. 'I am unaccustomed to this sort of thing. You must be patient with me.'

The huntress handed her a pair of riding gloves and said easily, 'We have all day.'

Afterwards, Ash would remember that first ride less for the awkward way she mounted Jewel – she had to climb on with one foot propped onto the lower bar of the gate – or for her novice's mistakes that sometimes made the whole endeavour quite painful, but for the way the ride made her feel like she might, one day, be free. It did not feel so strange after all, this animal beneath her, ready to spring through the forest. The work of keeping herself on the horse, every muscle attuned — however inexpertly — to the feel of the ground through Jewel's strides, seemed to dispel her nerves. Beside her the huntress was relaxed and calm, encouraging her without treating her like a child, and Ash found that it wasn't so difficult to talk to her, after all.

They stopped at the riverbank to water the horses just before noon, and as Ash clumsily slid out of the saddle the huntress offered her a canteen, saying with a grin, 'I did not forget it today.'

Ash took it, drinking deeply, and then came to sit beside the huntress on a fallen log. She handed the canteen back to Kaisa and said, 'You are very generous.'

'It is only water, not wine,' Kaisa said dryly.

Ash smiled. 'That is not what I mean.'

'What do you mean, then?'

'I mean . . . I mean that I am nobody. I am not sure why you are . . .' Ash trailed off, hesitant to continue.

'Why I am here with you?' Kaisa suggested, and took a drink of water.

'Yes,' said Ash.

Kaisa shrugged and looked out at the river. 'I suppose it seemed as though you were being placed in my path time and time again.' She put the cap back on the canteen and looked at Ash. Kaisa's green eyes were

161

flecked with brown, and her lips were shining from the water. 'I wanted to find out why.'

Ash asked, 'Do you know the answer?'

The huntress replied, 'No, not yet.'

Ana returned from her visit to Royal Forge flush with triumph; she believed that Lord Rowan was in love with her, and she worked very hard to put herself in love with him, despite the fact that he was twenty years older than her. Clara did her part as well, praising the elegance of his handwriting when Ana showed her his letters, and Lady Isobel could find no fault with his country house – or his considerable fortune. So, to make sure that Lord Rowan could not forget her, Ana spent more and more nights in the City as a guest of her aunt. Sometimes Lady Isobel and Clara went with her, and sometimes they did not, but Ash was always left at home. She took care never to allow them to see how much she relished their absence.

When they were gone, she and Kaisa often rode together. As Ash grew more comfortable on horseback, Kaisa took her on more difficult trails through the Wood, and Jewel began to allow Ash to lead her instead of simply following the huntress's horse. Sometimes Ash brought food for them, and they would spread out their cloaks in a sheltered spot in the Wood and eat bread and cold meat and cheese. They talked about hunting, or the way that Ash had felt on Jewel that day, and eventually they talked about their own lives. After Ash told her about Lady Isobel and her stepsisters, Kaisa said, 'I am glad I never had any sisters.'

'Where is your family?' Ash asked.

'I am from the South,' Kaisa told her willingly. 'My family breeds hunting horses.'

'When did you become apprenticed to a huntress?' Ash asked.

'At twelve,' Kaisa said, 'to the huntress near my family's home.'

'Is she the one who told you that tale about Niamh?' Ash was lying on her side, her head propped up on one arm, looking at the huntress, who was lying on her back.

'Yes,' said Kaisa.

'How long were you apprenticed to her?'

'Four years,' Kaisa answered. 'And then I came here, as the apprentice to the King's Huntress, Taryn. She came to my village and chose me.'

'I remember the King's Huntress before you,' Ash said. 'She came to Quinn House once, when I was a child, during Yule.'

'Did she?' Kaisa said, turning her head to look at her. 'What do you remember about her?'

'She was . . . she frightened me at first,' Ash said. 'Her hunters came with her, of course, and they brought a bloody stag's head inside with them.'

Kaisa smiled. 'Taryn did like a bit of theatrics.'

'And then she told me a story about a huntress who

went to retrieve a stolen princess from the Fairy Queen.'

'Eilis and the Changeling,' Kaisa said. 'She did love that tale.'

'Why?'

'I think it was because Eilis proves them all wrong in the end,' Kaisa said. 'All those who had no faith in her – who said she was too young – were mistaken.' She turned her head to look at Ash and added, 'She even outwits the Fairy Queen.'

'I asked her…' Ash trailed off, hesitating, and looked down at the ground. Kaisa's shoulder was only a hand's breadth away from her.

'What?' Kaisa prompted.

'I asked her if she had ever seen a fairy,' Ash said, feeling somewhat embarrassed.

'What did she say?' Kaisa asked curiously.

'I think she said something vague – I am sure she didn't want to disappoint a child.'

Kaisa propped herself up on her elbow so that she was facing her. 'Well, even if she had seen a fairy, she would never have been able to let on that she had,' she said. There was a mischievous tone in her voice.

'Why not?'

'The office of the King's Huntress has many secrets,' Kaisa said, a smile tugging at the corners of her mouth. 'Any knowledge of fairies or magic, of course, must be kept closely to the vest.'

Looking at the huntress, Ash felt a surge of happiness

within herself, as if she were unwrapping an unexpected gift, and the realization of it sent a blush of pink across her cheeks. She looked away uncomfortably and asked, 'Why did she give up her place as King's Huntress?'

Kaisa said, 'She fell in love.'

'And she gave up hunting?' Ash was confused. 'Why would she do that?'

'Her lover asked her to,' Kaisa said, and there was a curious note in her voice that Ash did not understand. But before she could dwell on it, Kaisa said, 'Why don't we ride upriver today? We haven't been that way before.' She got up in one quick motion, extending her hand to Ash. Caught off-guard, Ash took it, and though Kaisa's grip was sure, she looked away, and Ash saw a rosy flush along the curl of her ear.

As summer advanced, the heat came heavy and damp, and Ash sweated through her day's work while her stepsisters sat crossly fanning themselves in the parlour. Ana's romance with Lord Rowan had stalled, for most of the Royal City had gone south to Seatown during the hottest part of the year, but Ana had not yet received an invitation from Lord Rowan – or anyone else – to visit them there. That meant that Ash could not leave the house either, so when the invitation arrived at last, just after midsummer, even Ash was excited to deliver it to her stepsister.

'Finally,' Ana said in relief, tearing open the letter in

the front hall. 'My aunt has invited us all for a fortnight to her villa in Seatown!' She looked at Ash, who was closing the front door, and added, 'Unfortunately you are not invited; my aunt already has a lady's maid and you are not needed.'

'I would expect nothing else,' Ash said, a bit sarcastically, but Ana did not even notice. Overjoyed at finally being able to go to Seatown, she had already run upstairs to tell her mother the news.

But when Ash was once again alone at Quinn House, days passed with no sign of the huntress, and Ash felt anxious and low. In the past, she and Kaisa had made plans when they could, and when they could not, Kaisa eventually came to the garden gate to find her. It was almost as though Kaisa had a sixth sense about it, for she never came when Lady Isobel was home. Ash didn't ask how she knew, afraid that if she drew attention to it, Kaisa would stop coming. It was better, Ash told herself, to let it be as it was, for it would surely end soon enough. But now it had been weeks since they had seen each other, and Ash wondered, her heart sinking, if it had been the last time.

After several days of waiting in the empty house, listening for any sound at the garden gate, she decided go for a walk, unable to stand being inside for another minute. It was a hot day, and she almost immediately regretted leaving without changing into a lighter dress. Sweat was sliding down her back even before she reached the trees, and the shade was not much cooler. At the deserted riverbank, she knelt on the ground in the full sun and cupped the cold water in her hands, drinking deeply. She splashed the water on her face and ran her wet hands through her hair, pulling it loose from the knot at the nape of her neck. She undid the top buttons of her dress and splashed the cool liquid on her skin, sighing in relief as it trickled down her neck. She did not hear the footsteps behind her, and when she stood and turned to go back into the shade she was startled to see Kaisa standing there.

'I thought I might find you here,' Kaisa said with an amused smile. She looked as if she had just done the same thing that Ash had done: Her black hair was damp from the river, her collar unbuttoned and wet, the skin of her throat pink from the heat.

'It is a hot day,' Ash said inadequately.

'It is indeed,' Kaisa agreed. 'I would suggest that you come into the shade.'

Ash did not know what to say, suddenly feeling shy, so she stood there at the very edge of the shade and looked down at the ground. Kaisa's dark brown boots were comfortably worn and scuffed, the leather lined and aged. In the silence between them the buzz of insects in the hot summer air seemed to crescendo: thousands of tiny wings beating. At last she looked up at the huntress, who was watching her with a curious expression on her face; when Ash met her gaze she thought she saw Kaisa colour slightly, but perhaps it was only the heat, for the air was sticky with it. Ash twisted up all the courage inside herself and said, 'I was waiting for you.' When the words came out of her they seemed to hang in the air in a cloud of desire, and the texture of them surprised even Ash.

Kaisa said gently, 'There was no one at your home.'

'They went to Seatown.' She could feel the summer heat surrounding her as if it were rising from her body, and she reached up and squeezed the last droplets of water from her hair.

'Why did you not go with them? It seems as though the whole City has gone there.'

'Ana said she had no need of me there,' Ash answered. 'And she thinks it is a hardship for me to stay here, in the heat. But I am glad that I stayed.' *Because I wanted to see you*, she almost added, but the words caught in her throat.

'I am glad, too,' Kaisa said. The quiet afternoon opened up between them like a woman stretching her limbs. Ash felt the water from her damp hair sliding down the back of her neck, but she was still suffused with heat.

Kaisa said, her tone carefully conversational: 'I dislike Seatown in the summer. It is all young ladies and their mothers, seeking out suitable husbands.'

Ash let out a laugh of recognition. 'That is what Ana went to do.'

The huntress smiled. 'Besides, I had work to do. Prince Aidan will be hunting with us this fall after several years away, and the King wishes to hold a great hunt at the beginning of the season. It is only a few weeks away.'

'Oh,' said Ash, feeling slightly disappointed. She suspected that once hunting season began, her days with Kaisa would end.

But Kaisa said, 'If you would like to ride with us, I would welcome you.' Ash was simultaneously overjoyed and worried – her stepmother would never give her permission – and her hands flew up to cover her mouth, but she could not contain her smile. Kaisa laughed at the expression on her face and said, 'I take it that means I can expect you to join us?'

'I will try,' Ash said, and at that moment, she had never wanted anything more in her life.

When Ana returned from Seatown, her cheeks were blooming with what Lady Isobel described as the invigorating sea air. As Ash unpacked Clara's trunks, her stepsister reported that progress had been made with Lord Rowan. 'He seemed quite intent on proposing this fall,' Clara said, 'but I am not sure if Ana will continue to entertain him.'

'Why not?' Ash asked, unfolding Clara's blue gown.

'Because everyone says that the King will announce that Prince Aidan shall choose a bride this year,' Clara explained. 'It was all anyone was talking about in Seatown.'

'Does Ana somehow think he will choose her?' Ash asked dryly.

Clara laughed. 'You have no faith in my sister's abilities to twist things to suit her desires.'

'If there is one thing I believe Ana capable of doing, it is that,' Ash said.

'All she needs,' Clara said, 'is for Lord Rowan to *believe* that she has a chance with the prince.'

'Why?'

'It will make him jealous, of course, and he will propose more quickly. You really have no idea how these things are done, do you?' Clara gave Ash a condescending smile, and Ash bristled.

'And you do?' Ash said. 'You are only fifteen.'

'The Queen was betrothed when she was fifteen,' Clara said.

Ash turned from the wardrobe and looked at Clara incredulously. 'Do you think that *you* will make the prince fall in love with you?'

Clara's cheeks turned pink and she looked slightly embarrassed, but she said indignantly, 'Why not? Everyone says the King is going to announce that Prince Aidan will choose from among all the eligible girls in the country. I am eligible.'

'Well, in that case so am I,' Ash said, 'but I doubt the prince will choose me.'

Clara gave her a strange look and said, 'You may be our servant now, but you are the daughter of a gentleman, and you must know that you are far prettier than Ana.' When Ash simply stared at her, dumbfounded, Clara said, 'It may not be your dream, Stepsister, but do not scoff at those who do dream of it.'

The next day a messenger came to deliver an invitation stamped with the royal seal, and Ash hovered in the doorway to the parlour as her stepmother unfolded the letter and read it. 'There will be a hunting party to open the season,' Lady Isobel said, scanning the notice, 'and afterwards we are invited to attend upon His Royal Highness at the Royal Pavilion in the King's Forest, where he shall make a special announcement.'

'When is the hunt?' Ash asked.

Her stepmother looked up at her and said, 'In a fortnight. What interest do you have in it?'

'Perhaps she wishes to present herself to Prince Aidan as a possible bride,' Ana said sarcastically, and Clara looked down at her embroidery, saying nothing.

Ash frowned at her. 'Don't be ridiculous,' she said.

'Ash, go and clean something,' her stepmother said, irritated. 'You have no call to be here.' She stood up and closed the parlour door in Ash's face, and Ash heard Ana break into laughter.

★ ★ ★

Sidhean met her that night by the side of the river, where she sat on a rounded boulder holding the medallion in her hand. For a moment she thought she had seen a glimmer of light in its depths, but it had quickly faded and now the stone seemed as black as the night sky. She did not hear him approach, but she felt him – the air shivered a bit before his arrival – and when she looked to her left he was standing there motionless, his hands behind his back as he looked down at the gurgling water. 'How do you know where I am?' she asked.

There was a small smile on his face as he said, 'Magic.'

She had not seen him since he had given her the medallion. Now, she realized that the part of her that had once been always aware of him had quieted. And yet, seeing him again, she felt something within her bending towards him as though drawn on threads pulled taut by his hands. But he did not come closer to her, and she had the distinct impression that he was holding himself back, even though his face was expressionless. He asked, 'What is your wish?'

Ash opened her mouth to reply, and hesitated. She had heard many tales about men and women who had been foolish enough to make wishes in the presence of fairies, and for a moment she wondered what she was getting herself into. Though Sidhean might grant her wish, she knew there would be a price to pay. In all the tales, the price for a life was a life – to bring back the dead, a newborn child would be given up. But what would be the price for a day of freedom? She told him, 'The huntress has invited me to ride with them on their first hunt of the season.'

'Ah,' he said, and she noted that he did not ask why she was invited, or how she had come to know the King's Huntress, and she suspected that he already knew – that he had known – what she would ask for.

'The prince has proclaimed that he will make some sort of announcement at the hunt,' she continued, 'and my stepmother and stepsisters will be there. I wish to go without them knowing.'

He stood there for a long moment in silence, and to her astonishment he had never looked more like an ordinary man – with his head bowed and his shoulders slumped, he seemed almost weary. At last she stood up and went to him, putting her hand on his arm, and he was very real: He wore linen, and it was as pale as the starlight, and when she pushed his hair out of his eyes it was as fine as silk. She looked up at his shadowed eyes and asked, 'If you grant my wish, will there be a price to pay?'

He reached for her hand and brought it to his lips, and he kissed her knuckles. She felt lightheaded then, as if she had drunk a very great deal of wine, and if he had not caught her she would have stumbled. But he held her steady and answered, 'There is a price for everything, Aisling.'

'What is this price?' she asked.

He said: 'You shall be mine. That is the oldest law between your people and mine. But you must agree to it freely; if you do not, then I will not grant your wish.' The way he spoke gave her the impression that he had said those words many times before.

With his hands on her shoulders, she could feel the pulsing of her blood within her as if it were rushing up to meet his skin, and the price did not seem so high. Part of her thought, *at last*, and that part would have given herself up at that very moment. In a trembling voice, she asked, 'When must you have payment?'

'You will know,' said Sidhean, 'when the time is right.'

'Then I wish it,' she said quickly, before she could lose her nerve. She felt his fingers tighten on her shoulders, and she wondered if he were imprinting himself on her: Would the mark of his hands be visible? For now they were surely bound together.

'So be it,' he said, and then he stepped away from her – she felt the absence of him like a black cloud blotting out the daylight – and he bowed, and that disconcerted her more than the knowledge that she would have to pay.

Several days before the grand hunt, Ash began to see wagons full of crates and rugs and rolled-up canvases driving down the road from West Riding into the

Wood. The shopkeepers in West Riding were nearly as thrilled as her stepsisters about the hunt, for it meant good business for them, and each time Ash visited the milliner's to pick up another frill or tassel for Ana or Clara, there was fresh gossip about what Prince Aidan would announce at the feast after the hunt. But though the entire village was abuzz with preparations, she did not see the huntress, and at times she wondered if she had imagined their conversation that hot day by the river.

There had been no sign of Sidhean since the night she had struck the bargain with him, either, and she wondered whether her wish really would be granted. Sometimes she hoped that it would not, for in the light of day, with her hands raw from scrubbing the stairs and her dress stained with wash water, it did not seem that she had made a wise choice. But the night before the hunt, after she had banked the kitchen fire and finished washing the supper dishes, she opened the kitchen door and sat down on the doorstep. She looked out at the twilight garden and felt a thin but bright thread of excitement within her. Tomorrow, she knew, her life would change.

14

Ash was awake well before dawn on the morning of the hunt. She slept fitfully all night, waking nearly every hour to see that it was still dark, and when she finally gave up on sleep she felt groggy and slow. She went into the kitchen to make tea, and as she waited for the water to boil she watched daylight creeping into the cracks around the shuttered windows. Just as she was taking down the teapot, there was a knocking on the kitchen door. She went to open it, apprehensive about what she might find. The early morning sky was flushed pink over the Wood, and the air smelled of the last of summer, that scent of slowly fading grasses combined with the first hint of cool winter. On the doorstep at her feet there was a satchel made of finely tooled leather, drawn shut with a gold silk rope. The tassels glowed in the morning light as if they were on fire.

Just then she heard the kettle begin to whistle, and she hurriedly picked up the satchel and brought it inside, leaving it on the kitchen table while she made her tea. Then she took the satchel into her bedchamber and emptied the bag onto her bed. There were riding breeches made of creamy leather and a tunic of dark green, embroidered at the cuffs and collar in rich gold thread that matched the pattern of leaves and vines tooled into the leather satchel. There was a brown hooded cloak made of light wool, and brown leather riding gloves, and at the bottom of the satchel there was a pair of riding boots finer than any shoes Ash had ever worn. She sat down on her bed and pulled the medallion out of her pocket, and looking at the luminous, smoky stone she whispered, 'Thank you, Sidhean.'

After she had dressed, she wound her hair up and pinned it tightly at the nape of her neck, and when she looked at herself in the square mirror hung on the back of her door, her eyes were unusually bright. She wondered how her absence from the house would be explained that day. She felt as though she had stepped into an enchantment, and her heart raced. She went outside, her new boots moulding to her feet as they touched the earth for the first time – as if they were feeling their way into existence – and waiting at the garden gate was a grey mare, her coat speckled with white on the right shoulder in a pattern of stars. The mare arched her neck as Ash approached, her brown eyes flecked with gold. Her saddle and bridle were made of fine, dark-brown leather, and the saddle blanket was woven of grey-and-white wool that nearly matched the horse's coat. In the corner of the blanket a name had been embroidered in black: *Saerla*. 'That must be you,' Ash said to the mare, and when she put her hand on Saerla's neck, she felt a deep sense of calm.

Before she departed, she looked back at the house, and there was a woman in white standing in the kitchen doorway. Startled, Ash went back up the path, and as she drew closer to the house she saw that the woman's face and hair and hands were ghostly pale, and she had eyes the colour of gold. Remembering the fairy woman pulling her into the enchanted circle, Ash felt a tingle of fear run down her spine.

'Do you have everything that you need, Aisling?' asked the woman, her voice rippling like the notes of a half-forgotten melody.

'Yes,' she answered.

The strange woman said, 'There is one thing you must remember: Those who know you will still recognize you. Do you understand?'

'Yes,' Ash said, and the woman turned to go back into the kitchen. 'But wait – what will – will my stepmother and stepsisters see you?'

'They will see what they wish to see,' the woman answered. 'Now, go.' And she closed the kitchen door behind her. Through the window, Ash could see her taking down plates and bowls and teacups, apparently preparing to serve her stepsisters and stepmother their breakfast. Ash went silently back to Saerla, who was watching her curiously. She put her foot in the stirrup and swung into the saddle, and when she was astride the horse she looked back at the house, but the woman could no longer be seen through the window.

She rode across the meadow, heading towards the main road into the King's Forest. She had ridden this way with Kaisa several times before, and she knew where the hunt was to be staged, but this morning she saw everything with new eyes. Fresh tracks showed that many wagons had passed this way recently, but in the early morning the path was empty but for her and Saerla. The horse moved with a smooth grace that told Ash she had been given a hunter of extraordinary skill to ride, and as they entered the King's Forest the mare raised her head and whinnied as if she were coming home. Ash rested one hand on the horse's muscular neck and felt the animal's moving body beneath her palm, and she saw herself riding with Sidhean one night, her hand on his waist and the moon shining coolly over a grand, glittering palace. She blinked, and the vision was gone. It was morning: The sun shone down in long beams of light, raising the dew from the ground in misty breaths that lingered in the hollows between tree roots.

Ash's first glimpse of the hunting camp was not of a grand open field, but of small tents pitched beneath the trees, and men and women in green and brown turning their heads to look at her as she rode past. She could sense when she was drawing near to the central hunting camp, for the tents became larger, and the people moving around them walked more briskly, as if they were on a schedule. At last the path turned and broadened into a large clearing in the forest, and on the far side of the clearing there rose a great pavillion, the walls striped in tan and blue, and from the pinnacle flew the King's standard. The canvas walls of the front of the pavilion were rolled up, and inside dozens of workers were laying down carpets over the grassy field. On one side of the clearing, hunting horses were tethered to a rope stretched from one tree to another, and their flanks gleamed bay and brown and black and grey in the sun, which was beginning to peek over the tops of the trees. One by one the horses turned their heads to look at Ash and Saerla, and Ash could feel the mare tense beneath her, but she merely arched her neck and let out her breath in a low whinny.

Opposite the line of horses, some of whom were being tended by men and women dressed in brown, several marquees had been erected, each of them with a flag flying at its peak, and many with their front canvases drawn aside like curtains. Inside some of the marquees she could see the men and women of the hunt in their green and brown liveries, and amid all the activity the sight hounds, with their whip-like bodies and velvety eyes, roamed free. Ash dismounted and led Saerla toward the line of hunting horses, where she found a young man dressed in brown with a dark green armband. She said, 'I am looking for the huntress; do you know where I might find her?'

He turned from currying one of the horses and looked at her inquisitively. 'Who are you?' he asked.

His question took her by surprise, and she realized that, of course, she was a stranger asking for admission to see the King's Huntress on the first day of the season's first grand hunt. She said, hoping that he would believe her, 'I am – my name is Ash. She invited me to join the hunt today.'

Perhaps it was her horse that convinced him, or her fine clothes, for it could not have been her words, but he merely shrugged toward the line of marquees. 'She's over there somewhere,' he said. 'I'm not sure where.'

'May I leave my horse here?' Ash asked.

He glanced at Saerla and said, 'She's a beauty.' He pointed towards the end of the line and said, 'Tether her down there. Does she need to be fed?'

'No,' Ash answered, for she did not know what a fairy horse disguised as an ordinary one would eat. 'But perhaps some water,' she said in an afterthought; water would do no harm, would it?

'I'll bring her some water,' the man said, and then turned back to his job.

'Thank you,' Ash said, and led Saerla down the line and tethered her next to a black gelding who laid his ears back when they approached, putting as much space between himself and the fairy steed as possible. Ash looped the reins over the rope, and then walked towards the line of marquees. The first was empty, and the second was closed off, the front flap tied shut. At the third, several men were sitting around a table, eating, and Ash hesitated outside until one of them looked up and caught her eye.

'I am looking for the King's Huntress,' she said to them. 'Can someone tell me where she is?'

One of the men stood up and said, 'I'll take you to her.' He was tall, dressed in hunting green, and his dark hair was streaked with grey. He led her down the row of marquees until they came to the second to last one, which was grander than the others. Inside there was a long table, part of it covered with maps of the Wood, and around the table several chairs were scattered. The huntress was standing at the end of the table talking with another young woman, who was dressed similarly in hunting green. At the other end of the table a man in black was seated, leaning back with his feet propped up on another chair. He looked over at Ash as she entered, and she saw that a thin but prominent scar ran down his left eyebrow and partway down his cheek.

'What have we here?' he asked, and when he spoke, Kaisa looked up.

'This woman is looking for you,' said Ash's escort to Kaisa.

Kaisa seemed surprised but pleased to see her. 'I was

not sure if you would come,' she said.

Ash was conscious of the other people in the marquee looking at her, and she felt constrained and shy. 'Thank you for inviting me,' she finally said, and Kaisa, who smiled at her, seemed to understand the reason for her awkwardness.

She turned to the man who had brought Ash to the tent and said, 'Thank you, Gregory. Has the lymer returned?'

'No,' he answered. 'I'll send him to you as soon as he does.'

'Thank you,' Kaisa said, and then the man nodded to her and left. She gestured toward the other woman and said, 'Ash, this is Lore, my apprentice.' Lore's dark blond hair was braided in a thick plait down her back, and she stepped towards Ash and extended her hand over the table, giving her a measuring look.

For a moment Ash hesitated, and in that moment she saw Lore's look change slightly, as if she found Ash amusing. Feeling as though she had something to prove, Ash reached out and grasped the apprentice's hand firmly and said, 'Good morning.'

'Good morning,' said Lore. 'You are the girl we saw in the forest that night, aren't you?'

Ash felt herself colouring a bit as she answered, 'Yes.'

Kaisa glanced at Lore out of the corner of her eye, but merely asked in a low voice, 'Will you need a horse today?'

'No,' Ash said. 'I have a horse with me – she is with the others.'

Kaisa raised an eyebrow, and Ash was nervous that she would ask her where she had acquired the horse – and her clothes – but she did not. Instead, she shifted the map that she had been examining on the table, and tapped her finger on the parchment. 'This is where we are,' she said. Ash came to stand next to the huntress and looked down at the map; Kaisa was pointing at a clearing in the southern part of the King's Forest. In the north, the trees trailed off the top of the map as if the Wood went on for ever. Quinn House was an irregular mark near the bottom, and there was the meadow, and the path from the meadow that led to the twisting line of the river.

'I sent the lymer out this morning with bloodhounds to find the stag I've been tracking,' Kaisa continued. 'He went north of us, and he should be back soon.'

Lore looked at Ash and asked, 'Have you hunted before?'

Ash glanced at Kaisa for guidance, but the huntress gave her no indication of what to say. 'This is my first hunt,' Ash finally answered.

Before Lore could respond, a thin, wiry man with a shock of red hair came into the marquee, and the man at the other end of the table stood up and said, 'At last! We've been waiting for you all morning. I'm eager to begin.'

'The stag moved farther than we expected, Your

Highness,' said the new arrival, and Ash realized that the man with the scar was Prince Aidan. She had expected someone much more elegant; this man wore black riding leathers and a black shirt that looked as if it had seen better days. The scar gave a war-like cast to his features, and Ash was surprised that her stepsisters had found him handsome.

The lymer came toward Kaisa and pointed to a spot on the map just off one of the thinly marked trails that disappeared in the north. 'It's a grand one,' he said. 'He'll give us a good chase.' He had found the stag about an hour's walk north of where they were camped, and he had marked the path to show them the way back.

'Good,' said Kaisa. 'Lore, please call everyone together so that we can begin.'

Outside, the dogs were being gathered together by the master of hounds, and as Ash walked with Kaisa and the prince toward the hunting horses, Ash asked, 'Will all the dogs be used today? There are so many.'

'The first relay of dogs will rouse the stag,' Kaisa explained. 'But the dogs will tire before the stag does, so we place additional relays of dogs along the trail to take over when the others are winded.'

'But how do you know where to send the dogs before the stag runs?' Ash asked.

'We don't, exactly. But we'll try to chase him in a particular direction, and at any rate, the stag will likely run straight, down the most direct path.'

Kaisa paused before going to her horse and said to Ash, 'You are welcome to ride with me, but I cannot wait for you.'

'I'll keep up,' Ash said. Kaisa was different this morning than she had been on their rides together. She was more forceful, yet more withdrawn. Over the summer she had been relaxed, easy; now she was more upright, somehow, as if the office of the King's Huntress made her stand taller.

And it was the King's Huntress who nodded to Ash and said before walking away, 'I am sure you will ride well.' Her words contained a confidence that made Ash feel an unexpected thrill of pride, for of course, Kaisa herself had taught her.

Saerla was eager to begin, and when Ash mounted, she could feel the mare's taut energy beneath her. She saw Kaisa raise her gloved hand and signal to the pennant bearer, and the hunters fell in line behind her as they rode out of the camp. Ahead of them Ash could see the lymer and his dogs running forward at an easy pace, their spotted coats of black and brown on white like sunlight dappling the ground through the foliage. They rode for the better part of an hour, until Kaisa halted them all to allow the lymer to go ahead on his own. Everyone was sitting forward now, tense and silent, and Ash felt the breeze on her skin bring a rush of blood to the surface. She was nervous.

When they heard the notes of the hunting horn,

Kaisa shouted at them to follow, and the hunters plunged forward through the trees with Kaisa in the lead. Ash felt Saerla's muscles bunch and stretch as they rode hard toward the sound of the horn, and though she had wondered if she would be afraid, she was not. She felt the thrill of the hunt coursing through her that morning with a sharp, bright focus, and all there was, was the ride itself – muscle and bone moving together, the wind snapping her cloak back, and the ground rolling past her as they went deeper into the Wood. When Ash looked ahead she saw a blur of green tunics and horseflesh moving through the trees, and there was Lore, her horse's black tail flying. Then she saw the dogs again and they were racing after the stag, his brown flanks flashing between the trunks. She recognized the way the stag sprinted through the trees as if it had been painted in a storybook. He would double back on his path and attempt to lose them in the river, and then the second relay of hounds would scent him out and once again plunge into the chase.

At the riverbank the stag splashed in the shallows but the river was too wide at this point for him to wade across, and with a wild look in his eyes he clambered up the bank away from the pursuing dogs, and Ash could see the white froth of sweat rising on his flanks. He was becoming tired, and Ash thought that he would not run for much longer. But once back under the shade of the trees the stag regained his momentum – or found a new desire to live – and the chase was renewed with vigour. Ash recognized the trails they were following; despite the time they had been riding they had not gone far, and it seemed that the stag had fled in circles. But she was surprised when she saw they were nearing the edge of the Wood, and the stag leapt ahead of them into the open meadow where, in the far distance, she saw Quinn House. The perspective was different, though; they had emerged from the trees south of where she normally entered the Wood. And then ahead of her, Kaisa had ridden up to the stag with her arm extended and there was a flash of steel and then red streaked down the stag's throat. It let out a cry that ended abruptly when Kaisa plunged the sword – for it was a sword she held up in the sun – down behind the front left leg and into the heart of the stag, and it fell onto the fading grass of the meadow, its magnificent rack of antlers lolling onto the ground like the weight of its life, spent.

Kaisa slid off her horse and went to the stag and pulled her sword free, and the stag's body shuddered once more. She knelt down near it and put her free hand on the stag's great head, touching it with a gentle hand, and closed her eyes and whispered something that Ash could not hear. Then she stood up and, with her sword, slit the belly of the stag open from its throat to its tail, and blood and innards spilled out into the mid-afternoon sun. She cut across the breast as well, and then from the vent up the inside of each of the stag's rear legs, and from within the mess that extruded from its belly Kaisa cut out the warm liver. She sliced off a generous portion and gave it to the lead bloodhound who was waiting patiently near the head of the fallen stag. The hound took it with a growl of appreciation, his teeth sinking deep into the flesh of the animal he had chased. Kaisa cut off another small piece of the liver and held it up in a bloody hand for the prince, who dismounted from his horse and knelt down on the ground before the huntress. She placed the flesh in his mouth, her fingers streaking dark red over his lips, and she marked his cheeks as well with crimson slashes.

Then the prince stood and turned to the hunting party that had circled around them and said, 'Let us all celebrate our success today!' He took the wineskin handed to him by the lymer and drank deeply, and a trickle of red wine slid down his throat, darker than the bright splashes of blood on his skin. The hunters let out a cheer, and Ash watched as Kaisa turned her back on them and wiped her sword off on the meadow grass. As the other riders dismounted and began to pass around the wineskin, Ash went to Kaisa, who still stood with her back turned to the others. She put a hand on the huntress's shoulder and asked, 'Is everything as it should be?'

There were tears in Kaisa's eyes, and they ran down her cheeks as she answered, 'Yes.' Ash looked back at the carcass of the stag, and saw that the dogs were being held off now, and one of the men was approaching with his kit of knives to begin the butchering.

'Why do you do this if it affects you so?' asked Ash.

Kaisa looked down at the ground and said, 'It is the way of life. It ends.'

Then Lore was standing beside her and said, 'Come, let us drink to our success.' She handed Ash the wineskin and Ash took a drink, and it was the taste of ripened grapes in the sunlight. When she swallowed, it coursed down her throat in a thick warm rush, and then she handed the wineskin to Kaisa, who took it and drank as well.

Ash asked, 'What happens now?'

Lore answered, 'The stag will be flayed and the carcass divided up, and then we'll head back to camp.'

Kaisa smiled and said, 'There will be a great celebration.'

Lore laughed. 'Indeed.'

15

By the time they were ready to ride back to camp, with the stag's carcass butchered and packed onto a cart, the sun was hanging low in the sky. The wine had made Ash feel woozy, and as they rode through the Wood the trees seemed to blur, as if the whole forest were melting into one great swath of dark green. From time to time Ash thought she saw the air split apart as if torn by an unseen hand, and within that secret space was the oldest land of all. As they neared the camp they passed torches planted upright on tall poles in the ground, and the burning flames steadily drove back those twilight shadows, leaving only the darkening Wood and the rising sound of laughter.

While they had been hunting, the guests that would attend that evening's celebration had arrived, and as the Royal Hunt rode into the clearing, a cheer arose from the crowd that had gathered along the path. Each of the marquees had been turned into a well-appointed waiting room furnished with rugs and chairs and pillows for those who had come to dine and to dance that night. The hunters gathered in a semi-circle facing what was now a central avenue leading to the grand pavillion, and Prince Aidan and Kaisa went forward to meet the King and Queen, bowing deeply to them. Then Kaisa turned to an attendant behind her and gestured for him to bring the stag's head, which was wrapped in a dark green cloth. She took it by the antlers and laid it on the ground at the foot of the King, and when she removed the green cloth the crowd gasped, for the head was an eerie sight in the torchlight.

The King reached out and grasped Kaisa's shoulder and said, 'Well done,' and she bowed her head to him. Then he said to all who were gathered: 'We shall celebrate tonight's success with a great feast. But we shall also celebrate my son's decision that by the time this year has come to a close, he will have chosen a bride.' The crowd shifted excitedly when the King said this, and Prince Aidan came to stand beside his father and mother.

'Beginning tonight,' the King continued, 'Prince Aidan shall search for a lady worthy of becoming his wife. We shall invite every eligible young woman to join us at a grand ball on Souls Night to deliver her suit to the prince, and by the time of the Yule celebrations, he will have made his decision.'

The crowd burst into whispered conversation until Queen Melisande, her golden hair swept up beneath a jewelled coronet, raised her hand to quiet them. She stepped forward and took the arm of her son, whose face, with the marks of the stag's blood like dark slashes in his cheeks, was downcast. 'Now, ladies,' the Queen began in a voice accented with the round vowels of a Concordian, 'please be advised that my son shall not be choosing only based on beauty, for I am sure that every young woman here tonight is beautiful enough to win his heart.' Laughter twittered through the gathered crowd, and the Queen continued, 'He must make a good match for this country, as well. He has told me that he wishes to take a bride from his own land, even though I have urged him to choose one of my own countrywomen.' The Queen frowned at her son, who gave her a weak smile.

'But Aidan has always been a stubborn boy and has grown into an even more stubborn man,' said the Queen, 'and so it is with a mother's loving heart that I bow to his wishes. I trust that my son will choose wisely and well.'

Prince Aidan leaned towards his mother and kissed her on the cheek, and though she could not be sure, Ash did not think that he seemed particularly thrilled by his parents' announcement.

After the horses had been watered and fed, Ash joined the rest of the Royal Hunt as they made their way toward the pavillion, where Kaisa had gone ahead with the royal family. Ash walked with Lore up the avenue, and Lore said to her, 'You rode well today.'

'Thank you,' Ash said, nonplussed, for Lore had not seemed to be particularly interested in befriending her.

'I admit I was surprised,' said the apprentice, grinning at her.

'Why?' asked Ash.

'You said that you had never ridden in a hunt before,' Lore said.

'I have been … practising,' Ash said.

Lore nodded. 'Kaisa told me.'

'She did?'

'She spent much more time here last summer than she has before,' Lore said. 'I wondered what was keeping her occupied.'

Ash looked at the apprentice, unsure of how to interpret the slightly teasing tone in her voice, but Lore had turned her face away, and they walked the rest of the way in silence.

During the hunt, the pavillion had been transformed into a great ballroom. The forest floor had been carpeted in rugs of dark brown patterned with leaves of gold, and at the north end of the pavillion a dais had been raised, upon which rested a long table covered in creamy linen. At the centre of the table were two massive, carved oak chairs, and the King and Queen were seated there. To their left was Prince Aidan and his younger brother, Prince Hugh, and to their right was Kaisa. The pavillion was lit with hundreds of lanterns hanging from the wooden ribs that held the pavillion's roof aloft: globes of light suspended in mid-air. Long, cushioned benches were set around the perimeters of the pavillion, and on the south end a trestle table was piled high with food for the guests, who were filling their plates with roasted meat and bread and steaming potatoes. Attendants carried pitchers of wine around the room, and on a smaller dais directly facing the entrance, musicians were playing.

Ash began to turn to the buffet table, but Lore touched her arm and said, 'No, come and sit with us.' They sat at one end of the King's table with the other members of the Royal Hunt and were served roasted game hens and rabbit, dark bread and rich butter, charred roasted potatoes and carrots, sharp cheese and ripe, sweet green pears. 'There will be venison,' said Lore, 'just when you think you've eaten too much.'

When most of the dishes had been served, Kaisa left her place at the centre of the table and came to sit with them, and Ash listened as they talked about the chase that day: which horses had done well, whether the lymer's oldest hound should be retired, their plans for this new season. Ash watched the huntress, who was gesturing with her left hand as she spoke, and the ring she wore – a gold signet ring stamped with the seal of the Royal Hunt – winked in the light. She glanced at

Ash in mid-sentence and Ash quickly looked away, feeling overwhelmed by it all: Kaisa, the hunters, the banquet hall, the King and Queen, barely twenty feet away from her. She stared down at the gold leaves embroidered on the cuffs of her shirt, and they seemed almost alive, as if they might grow into sinuous vines and twine themselves up her arm, making her sleeves of glittering foliage. She closed her eyes, willing herself to be rooted there, in that chair, and she gripped the armrest until the pattern carved in it rose up to meet her fingers, solid and reassuring. When she looked up again, the hunters were talking of Prince Aidan's recently announced quest for a bride, and Kaisa seemed just the smallest bit tired from the long day, and it was as ordinary as a royal feast could be.

After the venison, when the last of the food had finally been cleared away, Ash leaned back in her chair and wondered if she would ever be able to stand again. The musicians were playing a stately pavane, and she watched with heavy-lidded eyes as Prince Aidan and his brother descended from the dais to choose partners from among the young ladies fanning out before them like the brightly coloured feathers of a peacock's tail. Prince Aidan took the hand of a slight, golden-haired girl wearing a gown made of pale blue trimmed with black ribbons, and Prince Hugh chose a redhead in a black silk dress with diamonds at her throat. Then Kaisa left the dais, and as she began to make her way along the edge of the pavilion, she was met by a black-haired woman in a red dress, who put her hand on Kaisa's arm and smiled at her. Kaisa stopped, and Ash watched as the huntress led the woman toward one of the cushioned benches where they sat down together, and the woman leaned toward the huntress, the light shining over the curve of her lips.

Lore, who was still sitting at the table with Ash, said, 'There are many who would cast themselves as the huntress's lover.'

Ash looked at Lore, blinking slowly, for the wine made her feel as if she were walking through cobwebs. 'What do you mean?' Ash asked.

Lore smiled at her almost pityingly. 'I thought you were one of them,' Lore said.

Ash felt heat rise in her cheeks at Lore's words and asked, 'Why would you think that?' She wondered uncomfortably if she had done something to suggest it. And if she had – did she feel that way? The idea was unsettling; it made her feel vulnerable.

Lore had opened her mouth to respond, but then one of the hunters appeared on the other side of the table and said, 'Lore, come and dance with me, will you?' He saw Ash's reddened face and added, 'Unless you have other designs?'

Lore laughed at that and said, 'I'll dance with you, Gregory.' She pushed her chair back and followed him down to the dance floor. Relieved to be free of that conversation, Ash watched Lore and Gregory bow to each other before they entered into the elaborate roundelay that was in progress, the ladies' many-coloured gowns spinning outward like blooming roses scattered over the ground. Towards the centre of the pavillion she saw a woman dressed in bright pink, her hair woven with white ribbons, and when the gentleman she was dancing with spun her to face the dais, Ash realized the woman was her stepsister, Ana. Ash stiffened, but Ana had not seen her; all of her attention was focused on her dance partner, a middle-aged man with a balding head of greying hair. Ash looked around the perimeter of the pavillion until she found her stepmother and Clara seated on a bench on the far side of the dance floor. They were watching Ana as well, but Ash was too far away to see their expressions. She realized, when she looked around, that she was the only person remaining at the table; even the King and Queen were dancing. If she stayed, it was only a matter of time before her stepmother noticed her there. She knew, then, that she had to leave.

She stood up to go, and as she made her way towards the exit, skirting the borders of the dance floor, she saw the huntress in the crowd ahead of her. They came together amid the throngs of people dressed in crimson and purple and rich black velvet. 'You look as if you are leaving,' said Kaisa, and those around them turned to look at whom the King's Huntress spoke to.

'I am,' Ash answered, schooling her face into a blank expression so no one might read the tension within her. She worried that her stepmother would see her; she worried that Kaisa would somehow discern a new awareness in her, in the way she held herself, her body tilting slightly, self-consciously, away.

But Kaisa seemed merely disappointed. 'You will not stay?' she asked. 'There is much more dancing to be had.'

Ash shook her head. 'I am sorry. I must leave.'

'Then let me walk you to your horse,' said Kaisa, and Ash nodded. They went together through the dancers then, and when they exited the pavillion the night felt cool and dry. There were few people outside, and the torchlit path leading past the marquees was almost deserted.

'You rode well today,' Kaisa said.

'Thank you for allowing me to come with you,' Ash said formally.

'You must join us again. We will hunt tomorrow, and though the King and Queen will return to the City, the hunt will remain here for several weeks into the hunting season.'

'I will try,' Ash said.

They passed a couple walking back towards the pavillion arm in arm, the lady giggling as she held up her long skirts to avoid tripping over them on the uneven ground. When they were alone again Kaisa asked, 'Is something wrong?'

She spoke lightly, as if Ash were a nervous sight hound who might be spooked by a more serious tone, and Ash managed to say, 'No, of course not.' She wasn't exactly telling the truth, but she wasn't entirely lying, either, for she did not believe that *wrong* was an accurate description of her feelings. Perplexed, yes; uncertain, yes; but beneath it all something as yet unnamed was coming into focus.

They turned off the main path towards the working area of the hunting camp where the horses were tethered, and Kaisa said, 'I hope that you enjoyed yourself today.'

There was something in her voice that sounded the tiniest bit affronted, and Ash looked at the huntress and said quickly, 'Oh, I did – I will never forget today.'

The huntress let out her breath in a small laugh, and she said, 'I am glad.'

Afraid to let silence come up between them again, Ash asked clumsily, 'You said – you invited me – how long will you hunt this season?'

'I am not sure yet,' Kaisa answered. 'It will depend on how successful we are in the next few weeks.'

They reached the smaller path leading to the horses, and Kaisa stepped back to allow Ash to go ahead of her, as if she were a lady. Ash almost stopped, confused. And then she asked, to hide the quick rush of nerves in her belly, 'Have — have you ever lost a stag during a hunt?'

'Of course,' Kaisa said, following her onto the path, 'but not for many seasons. The last one I lost — he was a quick one. He crossed the river and took a path I did not know existed. It led into a ravine deep in the forest, and we could not follow.'

'Why could you not follow him?'

'There were too many hunters with me that day. It would have been impossible for us all to follow. But later I did go back to that place, and it was so strange — I found the path to the ravine; I know it was the right one because the branches had been broken by the stag's passage. But I could not find the ravine. It was as if it had vanished, and I kept tracking the stag's trail in circles until I gave up.'

'There is a story,' Ash said, 'of a stag that runs into a valley, and of the huntress who followed it.' They had reached the horses by then, and Ash went to re-saddle Saerla, who turned her moonlight coloured nose toward them as they approached.

'What did she find?' asked Kaisa.

'The entrance to the valley was hidden, but there was a secret entrance that was revealed only by the light of the full moon, and one night the huntress was watching that very location and she saw the entrance revealed. So she went in.'

'What happened when she went in?'

'In the valley there was a cave. Inside, it was like a palace made of gold, and the huntress walked down many richly appointed corridors before she came to what seemed to be a throne room. And on the throne was a woman dressed all in white, and she was incredibly beautiful, but she was also incredibly sad, because she had been cursed to spend her life locked in that cave, and the only time she could leave was as a stag.'

'What did the huntress do?' Kaisa asked.

Ash finished buckling the saddle in place and said, 'The woman asked the huntress to chase her down, as a stag, and to kill her. And then, she could finally be free.'

Kaisa asked, 'Is that your favourite fairy tale?'

'No,' Ash said.

'I would still like to hear it,' Kaisa said quietly, and the expression on her face was indistinct in the dark.

'I am not sure, any more, which my favourite is,' Ash said. The horse nudged her shoulder as if to remind her that she had to leave. 'I am sorry,' Ash said. 'I must go.'

Kaisa seemed about to ask her a question, but she did not. 'Safe journey home, then,' she said, stepping out of the way as Ash mounted the horse.

'Good night,' Ash said, and Saerla turned down the path that would lead away from the hunting camp.

'Good night,' said Kaisa, briefly bowing her head to her, and Ash was reminded, uncomfortably, of the bargain she had struck with Sidhean. It did not seem quite right to think of Sidhean and Kaisa at the same time – there was something disloyal about it. But though she tried to separate the two of them in her mind, she could not, for the bargain, she knew, included all three of them.

16

Ash dreamed that she was walking through the Wood at midsummer, and when she looked up through the canopy of leaves she felt the warmth and heat of the sun on her face. There was someone walking beside her, and she was not surprised to turn and see the huntress, who smiled at her and extended her hand, and Ash took it. Small white flowers bloomed all around them, and as they walked the flowers became vines that climbed up the tree trunks until it was as if the trees were hung with blossoms made of snow. When they came to a stop, Ash saw that the path ended on the edge of a cliff, and before them was a ravine. She could not see the other side, but the white flowers continued to twine down over the edge of the ravine like a rope ladder, and the huntress squeezed her hand and said, 'Shall we find that poor stag-princess?'

'Are you going to kill her?' Ash asked, and her voice sounded strange, as though she heard it from outside her body.

The huntress smiled and shook her head. 'No, but you will.'

Ash awoke, gasping, and sat up in the dim morning light in her small room behind the kitchen. There was a pounding on the front door, and from upstairs she heard a bell ringing. Dazed, she threw off the covers and dragged herself out of bed, pulling on her wrinkled dressing gown as she stumbled through the kitchen and front hall. Her stepmother was standing at the top of the stairs in the dim morning light and said crossly, 'Why aren't you awake? Someone is knocking on the door! Go and answer it.'

Blinking and bleary-eyed, Ash went to the front door and opened it, and the rising sun flooded into the hall, momentarily blinding her. A man was standing on the doorstep, holding out a sealed letter. 'I apologize for the early hour, madam,' he said, 'but we have many of these to deliver this morning.'

She took the letter he handed her and before she had a chance to reply, he bowed and retreated. She saw him mount a horse draped with the royal insignia and ride off, and then her stepmother called from upstairs, 'Close the door! You're letting a draft in. Who was it?'

Ash shut the door and looked down at the letter, but the light was too dim to make out the details of the seal. She took it to the bottom of the stairs and showed it to her stepmother. 'They brought a letter,' she said.

Lady Isobel came downstairs and took it from her,

handing Ash the candle to hold while she broke the seal. Ash watched her stepmother's eyes widen as she read, and a triumphant smile came over her face. 'How wonderful!' her stepmother cried.

'What is it?' Ash asked.

'The King has invited us to a masquerade on Souls Night,' Lady Isobel said with satisfaction. 'He says that I am to bring my daughters. Ana must have made a favourable impression on His Royal Highness at the hunt.' Lady Isobel took the candle and headed back upstairs, calling, 'Ana! Ana, wake up – you're going to be a queen!'

The night before, the house was dark when Ash returned home, and there was no trace of the woman with the golden eyes. She had taken off her fine hunting clothes and folded them into the trunk at the foot of her bed with the fairy cloak, but the next morning the clothes were gone. She shook out the cloak, wondering if the clothes had inexplicably become hidden beneath it, but only the medallion clattered out, the stone as opaque as ever.

It did not seem that her stepmother and stepsisters had noticed anything out of the ordinary the day before, and once the King's invitation arrived, all they could think of was this next ball, and the prince. They wrote to their aunt and cousins to consult on which colours to wear; they plotted over the first words they would say to

His Royal Highness when they were presented to him at the ball. 'One must be properly respectful and yet give a hint of playfulness,' Lady Isobel instructed her daughters over supper. 'It would do you well to recall that with all the gentlemen you meet. One cannot diminish the importance of this – you must always show that you admire his wealth and stature, but at the same time you must not be in too much awe of it.'

'Why not?' Clara asked. 'Do men not enjoy it when a woman is in awe of them?'

'Of course they do,' Ana put in, 'but you must avoid appearing as though you are interested only in his wealth.'

'Subtlety, my dear,' Lady Isobel admonished her. 'Remember to be subtle. He must know that you are comfortable with the luxuries in life, and yet at the same time you should not be *too* comfortable with them – after all, what will he give you if you seem to already have everything?' She laughed, and after a moment Ana joined in, but Clara seemed able to force only a thin smile.

That night as Ash was unlacing Clara from her corset and helping her prepare for bed, Ash offered, 'You don't have to do as they say, you know.'

Clara glanced at her stepsister out of the corner of her eye and said, 'That's quite something – for *you* to be telling me that.'

Ash frowned. 'You are in a better position than I am, Clara.'

'How so? I am the younger daughter of a gentlewoman with little to her name *but* her name – and I doubt that you understand just where the Quinn family ranks at court. It is not a position worth envying.'

'You have access,' Ash insisted, loosening the last of the laces. Clara raised her arms and Ash pulled the corset up over her head. 'You do not need to follow Ana's method of securing a future for yourself.'

'Access to what?' Clara asked, pulling her nightgown on.

'Access to … to court,' Ash said. Seeing her stepsister eye her sceptically, she rushed on. 'I only mean that you do not need to marry for wealth. You could do anything – on your own – you could earn your keep a different way.'

'How? I am a gentlewoman's daughter. I have no trade.' She turned to face her stepsister, hands on her hips, but she did not seem bitter. 'I do not deny that my mother and sister can be a bit . . . single-minded, but what would you have me do?'

Ash went to put the corset into the wardrobe, and said, 'I – you could – you could learn a trade. You could apprentice with . . . a merchant.'

'A merchant!' Clara exclaimed, as if the idea were ludicrous. 'Like your father?'

'I said apprentice, not marry,' Ash said sharply.

'I do not object to marrying well,' Clara said simply, and looked at Ash curiously. 'Do you?'

'I simply do not believe it is right to pursue someone because – because he is high-born, or has a station above yours, or can buy you a manor house in Royal Forge,' Ash said, increasingly impassioned. 'What if it does not end in the way you hoped for? You would only appear to be a grasping fool. And even worse, you would be … you would be *false*.'

Clara laughed. 'Not everyone can be as *true* as you seem to be,' she said, and the words were tinged with condescension.

Ash bristled at the tone in her stepsister's voice. She turned away to close the wardrobe door, asking tersely, 'Do you require anything else tonight?'

'No,' said Clara. But as Ash left, she called out, 'Don't be angry, Ash.'

Ash paused in the doorway, her back to her stepsister, and she wanted to tell her that she was *not* true; half her life was spent in secret. But even though part of her yearned to tell Clara – who had long been the closest thing she had to an ally in that house – about Kaisa, about Sidhean, she could not. She only said, 'Sleep well,' and left.

A fortnight after the invitation to the Souls Night ball had been delivered, Lady Isobel and her daughters left Ash at Quinn House while they went into the City. 'We will be home late,' Lady Isobel said to Ash when the carriage arrived, 'but I will expect you to be awake to attend us when we return.'

'Yes, Stepmother,' Ash said.

When they were gone, she went back to the kitchen where she had taken out flour and starter to bake bread. She began to work, but her mind was elsewhere. She had not gone back into the Wood since the night of the hunt, though the huntress's invitation had been direct enough. She had stayed home partly because her stepmother and stepsisters had been home as well, and by the time they were asleep it was too late, she told herself, to go to the hunting camp. But she knew that in reality, she was simply nervous – after what Lore had said – at the idea of seeing the huntress again.

As she waited for the dough to rise she sat on the back doorstep and looked out across the garden and the meadow, but there was no sound from the Wood today. If they hunted, they hunted far from here. She had a momentary panic that the Royal Hunt had packed up their tents and taken their horses back to the City, and she might never see them again. The worry got into her bread, and the loaves that came out of the oven that day were lumpy and dry. She looked at them as if they could speak to her, and perhaps they did; she covered the bread with a cheesecloth and took out the fairy cloak and went into the Wood.

It was late afternoon by then and it would be dark soon, for the days were growing shorter. Autumn filled the air with the slightly burnt scent of drying grasses, and the Wood was coloured as if it were on fire. When she reached the path that led to the central hunting camp, dusk was falling and shadows lay thick upon the ground. The torches that had been lit on the night of the ball were gone now, and the tents that had been erected on either side of the path had been packed away. Her panic flared up again, but when the path opened up into the broad meadow where the pavillion had stood that first night, there were still several marquees standing, and the hunting horses were staked out in the meadow where several men were building a bonfire. Ash approached one of them to ask for the huntress, and he took her to a marquee standing beyond the horses, calling out, 'Kaisa! A visitor for you.'

'Come in,' came the huntress's voice, and the man nodded to Ash before leaving her alone, standing before the heavy canvas flap that served as a door. Ash unhooked the rope that held it shut, and pushed it open. Inside, the huntress was sitting at a square table, where a silver pitcher sat near a goblet and the remains of a meal. A globe-shaped lantern hung from a hook on the central pole, and the floor of the tent was covered with a simple canvas cloth on which a red-and-brown rug had been laid. In the corner Ash saw a pallet, a trunk, and another chair. Kaisa seemed surprised to see her, and she put down the papers she had been reading and stood up.

'I am sorry to interrupt,' Ash said awkwardly.

'I was only looking at some notes … it isn't important,' Kaisa said. 'Come in and sit.' She moved the second chair to the table and set it across from hers, and Ash sat down, feeling as though she should have brought something – some of her misshapen bread? They looked at each other, and Kaisa's surprise was turning into something more measured; she seemed to be contemplating what to do.

'How has the hunting been?' Ash asked, wanting to fill the silence.

'We've done well,' Kaisa said. 'We may even finish early this season – I won't hunt more than is necessary.'

'Does the king demand more?'

'He demands enough. It is his son who demands more.' A troubled look passed over the huntress's face. 'He has been too long in the battlefield and does not know when enough life has been taken.'

'Is he ready, then, to choose a bride?' Ash asked, recalling the announcement that the queen had made.

Kaisa raised an eyebrow at her. 'So you've received the invitation to the ball on Souls Night?'

'The ladies of Quinn House received the invitation,' Ash clarified.

'Are not all eligible young ladies invited?' Kaisa pointed out, and grinned. 'Do you not share the desire of so many young ladies who wish to be his bride?'

She laughed, thinking of the way Ana and Clara would react to the idea that she might marry the prince.

'I would make a poor princess,' she said.

'Why?'

'Have *you* ever wished to be a princess?' Ash challenged her.

'That depends,' Kaisa said.

'On what?'

'On whether I would have to marry a prince,' she said, and her tone was lighthearted, inviting Ash to share her smile. At that moment the door was opened by a servant who entered to clear off the table. As he was loading the empty dishes onto his tray, Kaisa asked Ash, 'Have you eaten?'

'No, but —'

'Soren, bring a plate for my guest, and another goblet,' Kaisa said to the servant.

'It's not necessary,' Ash protested.

'It is done,' Kaisa said, and the servant bowed to them before he left. When they were alone again, the huntress asked, 'How are things, then, at Quinn House? Are you content?'

Ash laughed thinly. 'Content?' she repeated, and she heard the bitterness in her voice. 'I am a servant...' She trailed off, feeling uncomfortable; had the huntress not just sent her servant away to serve her? The difference in their stations had never bothered her before; in the Wood, when they were alone, she could imagine that they were at the same level. But after the hunt and the ball, she could no longer deny the bald facts of it. She

216

knew there was still a bit of flour trapped beneath her fingernails, remnants of her day's work; across from her, the huntress wore a ruby ring on her right hand, the stone glowing in the lamp light like a tiny fire.

'I am sorry,' said Kaisa, 'if I have offended you.'

She looked genuinely concerned, and Ash could only shake her head. 'Oh no,' she said. 'You have made me feel so welcome, as though I were the same as you and no servant at all; you have never offended me.' And then she wondered if she had said too much, and she coloured a little in embarrassment. She was saved by the return of the servant, who bowed to her too – thus deepening the flush on her cheeks – and set before her a plate of food as well as a gold-plated goblet.

'Thank you, Soren,' said the huntress. 'That will be all for tonight.' He nodded and left them, and the huntress picked up the silver pitcher and filled their goblets with wine. 'You should eat,' Kaisa said, 'before the food gets cold.' There was roast venison, of course, and flatbread, and sweet grilled onions and charred potatoes. It was so good that Ash had no trouble eating it all, and the huntress seemed pleased that she enjoyed it.

Something about the way Kaisa's face was lit by the hanging lamp reminded Ash of the great bonfire in the City Square at Yule, and she said, 'At Yule, when you and your hunters went to the Square – you sang a song. Where is it from?'

Kaisa took a sip of wine from her own goblet before

answering. 'That is a very old tune. Its origins are more legend than confirmed fact.'

'What is the legend?'

'It is said that many hundreds of years ago, when fairies still walked the land and the King's Huntress was appointed to go between both courts, a powerful greenwitch was called upon to cast a spell that would ensure the huntress's safe return each time she visited the fairy court. But in order for the spell to hold, each time the huntress went into that other world, she had to gather all of her hunters together to chant the words, for that would bind her to this world. If they ever did not say the spell together before she left for the fairy court, she might never be able to return.'

'And now it is sung only at Yule?' Ash asked, taking a sip of the wine, which was light and cool.

Kaisa nodded. 'As far as I know, yes.'

'Why?'

She shrugged. 'I am not sure. It is tradition. I believe that the huntress was called to the fairy court annually – at least this is what the stories say – and that annual visit was shortly after Yule, near the first of the new year. Perhaps that is why the song is still sung today at that time.'

'You speak of the fairy court as if you believe in it,' Ash said, taken aback.

'I will not discount anything that has endured in our traditions for so long,' said Kaisa, with a small grin.

'Does the King share your views?'

'He . . . he does not hold much with the old ways,' Kaisa said slowly. 'But I am free to do as I must to tend the King's Forest.' She paused, watching Ash finish the last of the venison, and then said, 'On the subject of traditions . . . you have never told me your favourite fairy tale.'

Ash grimaced slightly. 'I am not sure if it is my favourite any more, but when I was younger I would read it over and over.' She hesitated before she began the tale, wondering if it might reveal something about her that she wished to keep secret. But perhaps the wine had loosened her tongue, for it did not seem so unusual to sit there across from the King's Huntress and tell her the tale of Kathleen, a girl who wandered into a fairy ring and longed so much to return to that world that she left this one behind.

Kaisa listened intently, and when Ash was finished she said, 'That was not a particularly happy tale.'

'No,' Ash agreed, 'but I think that few of them are.'

'Why is that?'

'I think that they are meant to be lessons.'

'For children?'

'For life,' said Ash. 'Do not be seduced by false glamour; do not shirk your duties; do not wander off alone into the Wood at night.' As she spoke she thought wryly, *not that I've always followed those rules*.

'Do not fall in love with those who cannot love you,'

added the huntress. 'Did you learn from those lessons?'

'Not all of them,' Ash said. 'Did you?'

'I believe,' said Kaisa, 'that I am still learning.' This time when they fell into silence, Ash did not feel the need to fill it with questions. Somehow during the course of the evening things had shifted, and it was just like it had been when they had ridden together in the hot summer. They could hear the sounds from the bonfire outside – the laughter of men and women, snatches of conversations about hunting. Ash had been fingering the stem of her goblet, looking at its fine workmanship, when Kaisa asked, 'Will you come to the ball?'

She raised her eyes, and there was a warmth, an invitation, in Kaisa's face that she had not expected. She felt herself respond to it, a flush of heat rising inside her. 'The Souls Night ball?' she said, her mouth going dry.

Kaisa nodded. 'Yes. Will you come?'

'I – I don't know,' Ash stammered.

'I would like to see you there,' Kaisa said, and her voice was gentle.

Ash did not know what to say. She felt as though she had stepped into someone else's shoes – for surely the King's Huntress could not mean to invite *her*? But Kaisa did not seem confused, and she was waiting for an answer, so Ash said, 'I will try.' And then she realized that it was late and she had to return home to wait for her stepmother, and she rose from the table so quickly that she banged her hip on it. 'I am sorry; I have to go home,' she explained. 'Thank you so much for the food, and for allowing me to interrupt your evening.'

Kaisa stood up as well, and she stepped forward and took Ash's hands in hers and kissed her on both cheeks. 'Good evening, then,' Kaisa said.

Ash was momentarily astonished, for the huntress had never done that before, though it was the customary farewell practised by the people in that country, and her cheeks burned. 'Good evening,' she managed to say, and Kaisa pulled back the door for her politely, and Ash stepped out into the chilly night. Her legs felt slightly wobbly, but she told herself it was from the wine, and the cold air was welcome on her skin.

On the way home, Sidhean fell into step beside her, and for the first time in a long time, she was startled by his arrival. But when she saw him, his presence flooded into her; it was like ink being released into water, and it was a relief, for it was familiar. She put her hand on his arm and let him lead her off the path and towards the river, where the water rushed by with the half-moon wavering in the moving surface. They stood together for long moments without speaking, breathing in the cool night air. She felt him take her hand and press something into her palm, and when she looked down she saw a ring set with a moonstone.

'Why are you giving me this?' she asked.

'You are as deserving of fine jewels as any princess,'

he said, and when she looked at him the moonlight skipped off his face as if it were a mirror, and she could not see his expression. She held the ring up to the pale light and it glimmered with a slow, white, fairy's fire, and she knew that it was full of magic. There was more to this ring than mere ornamentation. He said, 'I cannot allow you to forget our agreement.'

'I would never forget,' she said, her voice strained, for she found it difficult to speak when he was so close to her.

'Put it on,' he said, and she could only obey him. When she slipped it on her finger, she had the disquieting sensation that she was being swallowed by him, that he was all around her, and though it was uncanny, it was not entirely unpleasant. In fact, in some ways it was strangely exhilarating, and she shivered. He caressed her cheek with his fingers, and she covered his hand with hers so that the ring was touching him, too.

'It is too much,' she managed to say, breathless.

He was rubbing her hands between his, and he said, 'It is only an adjustment. Now, you see? It is easier.' Gradually, the sensation eased a bit – she no longer felt as though all she could see was Sidhean, and his features swam into focus before her. It felt, now, as though he made more sense to her, as if the ring were binding her to him. He smoothed her hair back from her face, cupping her chin in his hands, and she was forced to look up at him, his eyes like crystals glittering in the dark. 'I do not trust human girls,' he said, and there was a cruel tone in his voice that she had not heard in years. He abruptly let go of her and she crumpled down to her knees, her breath rasping in her lungs.

'Did you trust my mother?' she demanded, for his words had awakened a small flicker of anger in her, and she fought back her fear of him with it.

'Your mother!' he roared, and she felt the blast of his frustration radiating out from him like a bonfire. She raised her arm as if to defend herself, but as quickly as his fury had erupted it was choked off, and he was holding himself up against a nearby tree as if he could not stand without it. 'Your mother,' he said in a calmer voice, 'has nothing to do with our agreement.'

Though he seemed weakened, she stood as if pulled by him, and he straightened up and drew her into his arms. She felt her chest heave; she was afraid she was going to cry. She felt the pulse of his body beneath her cheek, pressed against the fastenings of his cloak, and she realized for the first time that he wore a cloak that night – it was nearing winter, and the thought that he might need the warmth as much as she did made her feel grounded, relieved. It gave her the courage to say, 'I have another wish,' though she knew that if one wish were foolish, a second was far more dangerous.

She felt the rumble of his voice beneath her cheek as he asked, 'What do you wish for, Aisling?'

'I wish to go to the masquerade on Souls Night,' she

said in a small voice.

He reached up and stroked her hair, and said, 'You have still not paid for your first wish.'

'I will pay,' she insisted. 'But please, I beg you, grant me this second wish.'

With a sigh, he stepped back from her and held her at arm's length. 'So be it,' he said.

'Thank you,' she whispered.

'The enchantment will be weaker, this time, for you will be farther from the Wood,' he said. 'It will end at midnight, so you must return home before then.' He bowed his head. 'You must go home. It is time.'

'Sidhean,' she began, but he was gone before she even finished saying his name. Just as it always had, his sudden departure left an ache inside her: Every time, it felt like he took a part of her with him.

17

The morning of the Souls Night masquerade dawned with an unusual fog, and when Ash went out into the garden to pump water for her stepsisters' baths, the King's Forest was invisible behind the cool white mist. It burned off during the course of the morning, and each time she went back outside to empty dirtied bathwater into the meadow, she could see a bit farther, until at last, by noon, the sun was clear and cold above. After lunch, Ash helped Ana into her gown, a green-and-blue velvet dress with a high collar and a feather trimmed skirt. When Ana held the feathered mask over her eyes, she looked like a peacock. Clara wore a dress of brown and cream velvet, and her feathered mask, in comparison, made her look like a sparrow. Ash spent longer than she should have braiding small pearls into Clara's hair, so that when Jonas drove into the courtyard with their carriage, they were late. Just before sunset, they left to dine with their cousins in the City before continuing on to the masquerade at the palace.

Ash closed the door behind them and went back into the kitchen, rubbing her hands over her face. She had just begun washing the dishes that were stacked in the sink when there was a knock on the back door. She dried her hands off, took a deep breath, and went to open it. Once again, there was a satchel sitting on the doorstep. This time, it was made of blue velvet tied shut with a fine silver chain; on the ends of the chain dangled sapphire baubles. She picked it up and brought it into her room, where she poured the contents out onto her bed. An ice-blue silk dress flooded out over her patchwork coverlet like a rush of cool water. The bodice was embroidered with hundreds of tiny crystal beads in a complex pattern of flowers, and in the dusky light that came through the window, the bodice shimmered like the scales of a fish.

She took off her faded brown dress and put on the new one, and it felt like wearing the weight of spring: soft and warm, with the breath of an evening breeze over her skin. There were shoes, as well – satin slippers in the same ice blue – and a mask shaped like a butterfly, embedded with what seemed to be hundreds of tiny diamonds and sapphires. There was a shimmering silver rope studded with diamonds that she braided into her hair, and there were diamond pins to fasten her hair in place. At the bottom of the satchel was a black wooden box, and inside on a bed of velvet was a necklace in the shape of a diamond cobweb with a great sapphire at its centre. She put it on and looked at herself in the small mirror on the back of her door, and the jewels blazed with an unearthly light, shedding a pale, cold glow over her face. She put on the mask, which was tied with a silken cord so thin she could barely see it, and at last she took out her moonstone ring and slipped it on her right hand. She had a fleeting sensation of eyes on her – Sidhean's eyes – but when she blinked the feeling was gone, and the ring was only a ring.

She was ready when she heard the knock on the front door. She opened it to find a slender, short man who came barely to her shoulder. He was dressed all in white, and in the light of the lantern he held, his eyes glittered gold. He said to her in a strangely accented voice, 'We are here to bring to you to the ball.' Behind him in the courtyard stood an elegant carriage drawn by a pair of matched white horses. A footman stood waiting near the carriage door, dressed like the man in front of her. She knew that they were no more human than the woman she had seen in her kitchen on the day of the hunt, but this time, she did not have any desire to ask questions.

She came outside and closed the door behind her, allowing the footman to help her into the carriage. She felt the carriage shift slightly as the driver and the footman stepped onto the driver's seat, and then they were off, moving more smoothly than any carriage she had ever ridden in before. The seat was upholstered in white satin, and though it was a cool night, the interior of the carriage was warm as summer. She looked out the window, but she could see nothing; even when she pressed her face to the glass there was only dark outside, and she could hear no passing sounds. They travelled quickly, for it seemed to be scarcely a quarter of an hour before the carriage pulled to a stop and the footman leapt off his perch to open the door for her. She stepped out into the palace courtyard, which was filled with a great many carriages and lit by hundreds of globe-shaped lanterns hanging high overhead. The palace doors were open, and light and sound came at her in a great torrent after the silence of the carriage ride. The masquerade had already begun.

She turned back to the driver to thank him, and he said to her, 'Do not forget: All this will end at midnight.'

'I will not forget,' she told him, and then the footman stepped back onto his perch, and the small white carriage rolled away through the crowded courtyard and vanished through the main gates.

She turned back towards the palace and took a deep breath to steady herself, and then she walked carefully through the crowd of carriages and up the steps to the grand, open doors. As she went into the entry hall, those she passed turned to look at her, and many of them whispered about her in her wake, for none had ever before seen a gown such as hers. She went up the wide marble steps at the end of the hall and passed a set of huge mirrors hanging on the wall that reflected the burning light of the chandeliers. She paused and looked at her reflection in those mirrors, and she could barely recognize herself. The glittering mask over her face and the diamonds around her neck were luminous, and her dress seemed to float over the floor. She looked, she thought, like a fairy woman, and when she raised her hand to touch her face to make sure she was still flesh and blood, she saw the moonstone ring glowing as hot as fire.

She swallowed and turned toward the ballroom, hesitating in the grand doorway to stare at the spectacle ahead of her. The room was hung with silver and gold garlands and heaps of white hothouse camellias. There were hundreds of people dressed in crimson and gold and emerald dancing to the music of flutes and pipes. Directly across from her on the other side of the ballroom, tall glass doors led into the cool night. She had never seen so many people in her life, and she felt overwhelmed, for it seemed that a good many of them were staring at her as she stood there in the doorway of the ballroom in her glimmering fairy gown, searching for the King's Huntress. When someone came up the stairs towards her and bowed, she did not realize that he was bowing to her until he asked, 'Would you like to dance?'

He wore a blue and red uniform with elegantly polished black boots, and his epaulets gleamed gold. He extended a hand to her, and she said in sudden realization, 'I do not know how to dance.'

He smiled at her beneath his mask that looked like the face of a hawk – or at least, his mouth curved upwards. 'Let me show you how,' he said, and again he extended his hand to her.

In something of a daze, she took his hand and allowed him to lead her down the steps. As they descended to the dance floor, the crowd parted, and the guests in all their multicoloured gowns and glittering masks stepped back to watch them take a position in the centre of the floor. Her partner bowed to her, and following his lead, she curtsied, and the musicians began to play. Somehow she managed to copy his steps, and as more and more people began to join in the roundelay, it seemed as if her shoes were leading her along, telling her feet and legs where to move. It was a bit unsettling, and as she turned she could feel the gown swirling around her like wings trying to lift off, but her stolid, uncompromising humanity was weighting her down in an eerie battle. When the dance finally concluded, she bowed to the man with relief, for she did not enjoy the feeling that her shoes knew more about dancing than she did.

But her partner had not noticed her discomfort, and he said, 'You are a beautiful dancer.' He offered her his arm as he escorted her off the dance floor. 'Will you come and have some refreshment?'

'All right,' she answered, and as they walked off the dance floor she wondered why so many people were looking at them. He led her through the tall glass doors and out into the chilly night. They walked across a courtyard paved in white stones, past a fountain shaped like a horse and rider, and towards a grand glass conservatory, lit from within by hanging lanterns.

The guards standing outside the entrance to the conservatory bowed to them as they approached and then opened the door, and Ash realized, suddenly, that the man she had danced with was Prince Aidan, for he wore the royal crest on his shoulder, and when he spoke to her, she remembered, at last, the sound of his voice. 'Only my special guests are allowed to enter here,' he said to her, and inside the conservatory was a wonderland of blooming flowers and greenery, and the air was warm from the braziers that were placed down the centre gravel aisle. On either side of the path were cushioned couches, and all around were potted plants: artfully trimmed orange trees, flowering camellias, white roses twining up lattices along the glass walls. On the couches and along the paths, there were ladies dressed in gowns of many different colours, their feathered headdresses studded with jewels, and as Ash and Prince Aidan walked down the path, they all turned to look at her. He took her to an armchair and said, 'Will you rest for a moment? I will return shortly.'

Ash nodded and sat down. The prince bowed to her

and departed, and she watched him proceed down the path, greeting those he knew along the way. There was still no sign of Kaisa. She looked down at her hands to avoid the people who stared at her, and saw that the hanging lanterns were reflected in her ring like small embers. She felt awkward and ungainly and grateful for the mask that hid her face, and she felt Sidhean's magic all around her in a way she had not felt on the day of the hunt. Perhaps she was far enough away, now, from the Wood that the magic had to be stronger – or perhaps it was this gown, for she felt it must have been worn before by some fairy princess who once lived in an immense palace built of crystal and gold. It was as if she had slipped into someone else's skin, and it did not quite fit.

Thoroughly discomfited, Ash left her seat rather than wait for Prince Aidan to return. She walked in the opposite direction that he had gone and turned off the central aisle as quickly as she could, making her way past seated couples and boxes of rosebushes. At last she found an exit, and she pushed open the glass door and escaped outside, relieved to be away from the prying eyes of those who had watched her departing. She closed the door behind her and looked around. She was on a brick path that led away from the conservatory, and on either side of the path hedges grew to the height of her shoulders. With no other choice, she went forward and followed the path until it ended in a door in a wall. She reached out and put her hand on the cold brass handle, and it opened into a corridor lit with candles placed in pewter sconces moulded into the shapes of tree branches. She was inside the palace again, but she did not know where; the corridor was empty but for her and the shadows made by the flickering candlelight.

Her footsteps were loud on the flagstones as she walked down the corridor. On the wood-panelled walls hung portraits of women dressed in hunting gear, some sitting astride grand horses, some standing stiffly in the foreground of a wooded landscape, and one, with her long blond braid flying out behind her, raising a sword to a rearing stag. The corridor ended in a circular chamber with two black doors on the far side, and to her right, an archway revealed another corridor that turned a corner to an unseen destination. On the floor of the circular chamber, the tiles were inlaid with the image of a horse and rider facing a bowed stag, and as Ash walked around the image, looking at the skill with which the horse's eye had been shaped, one of the doors opened, and Kaisa emerged. She seemed surprised to see Ash there and said, 'Are you lost, madam?'

Ash realized that the huntress did not recognize her, for she was wearing the mask still. 'No,' she said in relief. 'I was looking for you.'

Kaisa came toward her curiously, recognition dawning in her. 'Ash?' she asked.

'Yes,' said Ash. She could see the hollow in the

huntress's throat, now, where the collar of her shirt was open; her skin was coloured gold in the candlelight. She came closer to Ash and lifted her hands to the mask, and when the cuffs of Kaisa's shirt fell back, Ash saw the glint of silver on the huntress's wrist before she untied the silk cord that held the mask to Ash's face.

When Kaisa stepped back and saw her, she raised her eyebrows and said, 'What a gown you are wearing.'

Without the mask, Ash felt self-conscious; she was not sure if Kaisa had ever looked at her like that before. She held out her hand to take the mask back, but Kaisa did not give it to her. 'Let me have it back,' Ash said.

'I prefer to see the face of the person I am talking to,' said Kaisa.

'Then you must not enjoy the masquerade.'

The huntress shook her head. 'Not especially. I feel that there are so many opportunities for slights – perceived or real – when we do not know who we are with.'

'You don't enjoy the mystery of it?'

'There are other mysteries I prefer,' Kaisa said, and then she returned the mask to Ash, who took it but did not put it on. 'Shall we go back to the ball?' Kaisa asked. 'I am sorry I was not there to greet you.'

Ash laughed nervously. 'I can go back … but I must wear my mask.'

'I suppose it is a masquerade,' Kaisa admitted.

'Do you not have a mask?' Ash asked. The huntress

234

wore a dark green shirt, the sleeves laced together with a brown cord from elbow to wrist, and brown breeches with shining boots, but she did not carry a mask.

She shook her head. 'I don't like them.' She gestured toward the corridor that led away from where Ash had come from. 'Shall we go?' This corridor was also panelled in wood, but after a short stretch it opened into a wider hall, lit with hanging chandeliers. It was empty but for the two of them. 'Why were you in the conservatory?' Kaisa asked as they walked.

'I was with Prince Aidan,' Ash began.

'You were with the prince?' Kaisa said incredulously.

'It is not what you think,' Ash objected, laughing. 'He – he asked me to dance. He did not know who I was. Then he took me to the conservatory.'

'Did you tell him who you are?' Kaisa asked.

'No, I – I left,' Ash said, sounding rueful.

The huntress laughed. 'This is why masks lead to trouble,' she said.

Ash had a sudden, horrifying thought, and she said, 'Please – don't tell him who I am.'

'Why not? Are you afraid it will ruin your reputation?'

Ash laughed in spite of herself. 'Of course not,' she said, 'but if my stepmother hears of it ... it will do me no good.'

Kaisa seemed amused. 'Do you truly believe that Lady Isobel's opinion would matter more than Prince Aidan's?'

'You don't know her as well as I do,' Ash said grimly. 'Just – let Prince Aidan remain in the dark about *one* of his dance partners tonight.'

Kaisa's mouth twitched in a smile. 'All right,' she relented. 'He shall have this one mystery, then.'

As they approached the ball they began to hear the music drifting down the corridor, and when they turned the corner they came to a balcony overlooking the ballroom. Ash went to the edge of the balcony and looked down at the dancers, and Kaisa came and stood beside her, leaning on the wide marble balustrade. 'It is quite a sight,' Ash said.

'Indeed,' said the huntress. 'But your gown puts all of theirs to shame,' she added with a smile.

Ash was embarrassed. 'It . . . is not mine,' she said.

'Whose is it?' Kaisa asked. 'The Queen's?' She straightened up and reached out to touch the jewels around Ash's neck, her fingers warm against her skin. 'These are worth more than a fortune,' she said. Then she moved away, stepping back and crossing her arms, and gave Ash an appraising look. 'You look beautiful,' she said, and Ash could not meet her eyes. 'But the dress does not suit you.' The warmth that had flooded through her when Kaisa had touched her twisted; she felt her cheeks flaming. 'It looks like it is suffocating you,' Kaisa continued. 'Who gave you this gown – and that horse you rode to the hunt? You must have a wealthy benefactor.'

'I . . . yes,' Ash said. She was not sure if she could speak of it, not directly.

'It frightens you,' Kaisa observed.

Ash knew she could not conceal her fear; she felt a prickling sensation along her limbs where the fabric of the dress touched her, as if there were fingers prodding her to move. This gown and this night were the last she could ask of Sidhean; his magic was impatient for payment. She could feel him waiting, as if he were lurking just around the corner, watching her.

Kaisa came closer to her and took her left hand, the one that was not wearing the moonstone ring, for Ash had curled that one away behind her. The mask dangled between them, the cord twined in their fingers. 'Let me help you,' Kaisa said. 'You don't need to face it alone.'

Ash heard her speak the words, but it was as though she heard them very distantly, for the dress was still pulling on her, tugging her mind's eye back to Sidhean. Then the huntress drew Ash's right hand from behind her back, covering the moonstone ring with her warm, human fingers, and at last Ash felt her there, so close that she could feel the heat from her body. And she said, 'You cannot help me; I must finish this on my own.' *There is nothing you can do,* she thought. *I am the debt; not you.* For the first time, the consequence of her choice was devastatingly clear: fulfilling her contract with Sidhean meant that she would never see Kaisa again.

'Is it your stepmother?' Kaisa asked.

Ash laughed, for her stepmother's demands were insignificant in comparison to the enchantment she had tangled herself in. 'No,' she answered. 'It is nothing so simple.'

'Then what is it?'

'Please,' Ash said, 'I must do this alone. You do not need to concern yourself with me – I know you have more important things to attend to.'

Sadness washed over the huntress's face. 'Ash,' she said, 'I would do whatever I could to help you. How can I make you understand that?'

'But why?' she could not help but ask. 'I am no one – a servant in a poor household. What could I give you?'

Kaisa seemed taken aback. 'You don't need to give me anything,' she said. 'I offer because I care for you. I thought you felt the same way.'

'I do,' Ash said, and as she said it she knew that it was true. It frightened her more than the dress did, more than the bargain she had struck with Sidhean. It made her skin flush and her hands feel cold, and she had to look away from the huntress, whose eyes were so green at that moment it was like looking at leaves on a tree. Below the balcony, in the ballroom, the dancers whirled in their dresses that had been spun from ordinary human-made looms.

They heard the tolling of a bell, ringing slowly and deeply, and as the hours struck, Ash remembered that he time she had been granted that night was coming to an end. 'I must go,' Ash said, and she stepped away from Kaisa, pulling her hands away. When Kaisa's skin was no longer touching the moonstone ring, it flared into life again, burning as though it were angry at her.

Kaisa lifted her hand to Ash's chin, turning her face so that she had to look at her, and she was both hopeful and resigned. 'You would owe me nothing,' Kaisa said. 'But it is your decision to make.' Then she stepped back and took the mask out of Ash's hand, helping her to fit it back over her face.

They walked together in silence down the corridor, and when it opened into the great hall filled with revellers and laughter and light, the palace doors yawning open at the far end, the huntress stopped. 'I will bid you good night here,' she said. Once again she kissed her on both cheeks, but this time Ash kissed her as well, and she wondered when – or if – she would see her again.

'Goodnight,' Ash said, and then Kaisa turned away and went back into the ballroom. Ash walked the length of the great hall slowly, and as she passed the entrance to the ballroom she turned to look in on the sea of people, a blur of colour beneath the flaming chandeliers. Within the crowd she saw Kaisa, the sole unmasked celebrant, turn back to look at her, and it was as if another world was laid over the one she was in. She could see Kaisa and the dancers and the solid heft of the marble pillars, but over it all she could see another ballroom. In this one, the revellers were all dressed as she was, in gowns as light and filmy as butterfly wings, with jewels as delicate as cobwebs slicked with droplets of morning dew, and the music was wilder, as if played on instruments that had not yet been invented. Anchoring the two worlds together was Kaisa, who stood there for one moment looking back at her, and then continued on into the ballroom.

The two worlds slid apart again, and Ash could only see the palace that she stood in. The present rushed back into her as she saw, coming up the steps from the ballroom to the great hall, Lady Isobel, Ana, and Clara. Ash's stepmother was not wearing a mask, and she looked extremely vexed as she herded her daughters out toward the courtyard and the carriages. With a feeling of panic rising in her, Ash began to run towards the courtyard, realizing that she would need to overtake them in order to arrive home before they did. Outside there was a crush of people waiting for their carriages, and Ash pushed through them, disregarding their comments about her rudeness. But when she could see the line of carriages waiting to drive up to the palace doors, her heart sank, for she could not see hers. She stood there looking desperately into the crowd until someone dressed in royal livery approached and asked if he could help, but then she saw the little white carriage, inexplicably, at the head of the queue. The footman leapt down from his perch and opened the door for her and said, 'Hurry; we have very little time.'

She climbed into the carriage and he slammed the door after her, and there was scarcely time for him to jump back onto the driver's seat before they were moving again. They drove quickly, and once again she could see nothing more than a black square outside the window, but this time she could feel the road beneath them. The carriage jostled uncomfortably as they sped out of the City towards Quinn House, and she had to cling to the edge of the seat. The drive took longer this time as well, and she felt as though the magic were draining out of this night far too quickly. When the carriage came to a stop at last and the footman opened the door for her, they had arrived in the courtyard in front of Quinn House, which loomed dull and stony before her. She stepped out and began to thank the footman, but he was already jumping back up into his seat with the driver, who told her, 'Go quickly; they are almost here.' The driver chirruped at the horses, and within the blink of an eye they were gone, and Ash was left standing alone in the dark. She heard, quite distinctly, the sound of ordinary carriage wheels approaching.

She ran to the front door and fumbled with the knob, but her fingers slipped on it in her haste, and for a moment she could not open it. Just as she managed to push the door open, the carriage rolled into the courtyard, and the carriage lantern shone into the dark doorway. She heard the carriage door open and her stepmother say, 'Who is that?' Ash turned around to face them, and her stepmother was standing beside the carriage, the look of surprise on her face turning into anger. She came towards her, her black cloak flying back as she came into the house. 'Aisling,' her stepmother said in a cold voice, 'what are you doing?'

Ash felt as though her body had just gone numb, and she did not answer. She backed away from the front door, retreating into the dark hall, and her stepmother came after her, blocking the beam of light from the lantern that had thrown their shadows across the wall. 'Clara, come and light the candles,' Lady Isobel called to her daughter, and in a moment Clara came into the house. When the match flared up, Ash saw Clara looking frightened and uneasy. Ana was behind her, and when she recognized Ash, her curiosity twisted into a look of fury.

'What are you wearing?' Ana demanded, coming closer to her. Ash tried to back away but Ana reached out and grabbed her wrist, digging her nails into Ash's skin.

'Where did you get those clothes?' her stepmother asked.

'Mother,' said Ana, 'she is the one that they were talking about all night. She is the one who danced with Prince Aidan and then disappeared.'

'That can't be possible,' Lady Isobel said.

'Look at her,' Ana insisted. 'I recognize the gown. Look at it – look at this necklace!' Ana reached for the diamond necklace and yanked at it, pulling it from Ash's neck, and the delicate strands broke, the large sapphire clattering onto the floor.

Lady Isobel bent to pick up the jewel. 'Did you steal this?' she demanded. 'How did you get these jewels and this gown? Have you been stealing from me?'

'No,' Ash said.

'She must have been stealing,' Ana said. 'These are diamonds, Mother! How else could she afford a gown like this?'

Her stepmother came towards the two of them, and in the dim light she took the strand of diamonds from Ana's outstretched palm. She held them up to the candlelight and they glittered, cold and hard. She looked from the jewels to Ash, and then said, 'Where did you get these things?'

Ash did not answer. What did it matter if her stepmother thought she was a thief? Her time here would come to an end soon enough. Even when Ana put her hand on the collar of Ash's gown and ripped it from her, Ash did not feel her stepsister's nails against her skin. 'She has more jewels in her hair,' Ana was saying, and her stepsister began to pull at the silver rope braided into her hair. 'I can't get it out,' Ana said in frustration, and Ash put her hands over her head, backing away until her hip struck the doorway to the kitchen. Her stepmother came to her and grabbed her by the shoulders in a bruising grip and propelled her through the doorway.

'Sit down,' she commanded her, and pushed her towards the kitchen table. Ash knocked against the bench, wincing where it struck the backs of her knees. Her stepmother pulled out a pair of kitchen shears. 'You have no respect for me or for what I have done for you,' her stepmother said, her voice hard. 'I have fed and clothed you for so many years, and this is how you repay me – by stealing from me. You are an ungrateful bastard, and I wish I had never married your father.' Then she pulled at Ash's hair and began to cut out the jewels in savage, uneven slices. When she had extricated them all, she handed them to Ana, who was watching with a triumphant smirk on her face. Clara stood behind them both, and in the light of the single candle Ash could not tell whether Clara was happy or horror-struck. She looked down and saw that her hair lay in clumps all over her lap and on the floor, and she began to pick them up with slow, clumsy fingers.

'You can clean up later,' said her stepmother, who went to take the square mirror down from behind Ash's door, and held it in front of her. 'There – see how much better you look now that those jewels are gone? You were always too plain to wear anything so grand. You should never have tried to rise above your station.'

In the mirror, Ash saw a pale, expressionless face with

wide brown eyes, and where there had once been a smooth length of dark brown hair, now she saw ragged edges pointing every which way. She looked like a madwoman. She glanced up at her stepmother and said deliberately, 'Thank you. I think it suits me.'

Her stepmother exploded with anger. She slammed the mirror down on the table so hard that it cracked, and when she saw the crack she reached out and slapped Ash across the cheek. She caught the edge of Ash's lip with her signet ring and Ash knew that she had drawn blood, for she tasted it as it ran into her mouth. But she was not afraid any more, even when her stepmother yanked her up again and pushed her out the back door and down the cellar steps. Before her stepmother locked the door after her, she said, 'You'll starve in there before you speak to me like that again.' She heard the turn of the key in the lock – the well-oiled click of the tumbler falling into place – and then her stepmother slammed the kitchen door shut above her, and her footsteps retreated until, at last, there was silence.

18

In the darkness, Ash pressed her bruised face against the back of the cellar door, feeling the wood smooth and cold against her skin: such a thin and porous gatekeeper between herself and the outside world. She moved away from the door and felt her way across the cellar until she came to her father's trunks pushed against the far wall. She sat down, leaning against one of them, wrapping her arms around her knees. The cellar smelled of dirt and musty air and this year's apples.

She was finally beginning to feel the sting of her stepmother's slap across her cheek, and when she prodded at the corner of her lip with a careful tongue, she winced. Her stepmother had never locked her in the cellar for more than one night, for she needed Ash to work. But she was especially angry this time, and Ash was not sure how long she would be left there. She put a hand up to her hair and touched it gingerly; her head felt much lighter now. She ran her fingers through the uneven remains of her hair and noticed that she was still wearing the moonstone ring; Ana must not have noticed it. Turning the ring around on her finger, Ash decided that when she was out of the cellar she would finish what her stepmother had begun and cut the rest of her hair off. She felt buoyed by this thought, and wondered why she did not feel angry at her stepmother. She felt, instead, strangely indifferent. Her life upstairs did not matter anymore. It wasn't real to her. It wasn't what she had ever wanted.

Her mind was racing with memories of that night, and she did not expect to become tired. But eventually she grew drowsy, and she did not know she had nodded off until she awoke to the sound of the cellar door opening. She scrambled up in alarm, thinking it was her stepmother. But the doorway was empty, and moonlight spilled down the steps and flung a rectangle of watery white light on the cellar floor. She got up and went to the door, wondering if this were a dream, and when she stood in the doorway she saw a path laid out in moonlight, glowing, up the steps and across the kitchen garden and out into the meadow. She decided to follow it.

It led her into the Wood, and she saw the path winking far ahead of her like crushed diamonds. It wound through the trees and did not follow any ordinary trail that had been broken in by hunters or the deer they chased. This path meandered like a river of light, and as she walked, her feet kicked up tiny flecks of silver dust that hovered in the air. The path came to an end in a circular clearing, where she saw a crystal fountain in which a hawthorn tree made of diamonds rained clear water. Standing by the fountain was Sidhean.

He came towards her and lifted her chin in his hand, and she was reminded, painfully, of Kaisa. He said, 'She has hurt you.' At first she did not know who he was talking about, and she wanted to say, *No, she would never hurt me*. But then she realized he was only referring to her stepmother.

'It is nothing,' she said shortly. 'It will heal.'

He seemed to be somewhat surprised by the tone in her voice, but he only said, 'Come and eat, for I know that you are hungry.'

He gestured behind him to a small round table and a comfortable round chair – they looked like they had been carved whole out of ancient tree trunks – and on the table was laid out a feast for one. There was bread and cheese and fruits that looked so ripe they might be bursting with juice, and what looked like dark sweet cakes laced with cobwebs of sugar. She asked, 'If I eat that food, will I die?'

'No,' said Sidhean. 'That is not my wish.'

So she sat down at the table and picked up the crystal goblet and drank; it tasted like wine, but it was sweeter and lighter than any wine she had ever drunk before. She took a piece of bread from a loaf shaped like a clover leaf, and it was salty and rich and studded with nuts. There was a sharp, pungent cheese that crumbled when she bit into it, and there was a soft, creamy one that she spread over the bread. There was a knife with a smooth wooden handle, and she used it to peel the skin of a round, red fruit; inside was juicy orange flesh that tasted both sweet and tart. The cakes were light as air, with a heady, liquid centre that stuck to her fingers so that she had to lick them clean, and when she had finished eating there was a bowl of water and a cloth at her side with which to wash her hands.

'This is fairy food,' she finally said, after she had dried her hands.

'Yes,' he agreed, and now he was sitting in a similar chair across from her.

'Is it real?' she asked.

His face was in shadow, but she saw his lips curve as he smiled at her. 'Of course it is real. We are real, you know. We simply do not live in your world.'

'Am I no longer in my world?'

'Not right now, no. When you took the moonlight path you came to my world.'

'You brought me here,' said Ash. 'Why?'

'You told me a fairy tale once,' he said, 'and now I have one to tell you.' He flexed his fingers and folded them on his knee before continuing. 'Once, a long time ago, when magic was stronger in this land, our two races were much closer than they are now. In those days, there was a reason for us to take humans into our fold, because together we created a kind of balance that was good and necessary. But over the centuries, almost all the magic within your people has disappeared. We do not know why. At the same time, your people often chose to ignore their mortality. No one is more impressionable than young humans. They are fooled into thinking they can live forever, when in fact they are about to die.'

'I am not fooled,' Ash said.

'No,' he agreed. 'You are not. And once there was another girl who was not fooled. She was no ordinary girl; she knew all the old stories. I could feel her more clearly than any other girl I had encountered in many years, for the old magic was alive in her. It was slight, but it was enough to awaken my interest. I have taken countless human girls, but not for many of your lifetimes. There has been no reason, for your kind does nothing for my people any more, and my people are reaching the end of our own time. I cannot deny that we are not what we once were.'

'Nevertheless, there was an opportunity in this girl. I sent her many dreams to lure her into the Wood at night, but she did not come. Finally, on Midsummer's Eve, when our magic is strongest, I went to her home and called to her. She came to her window then, and when I asked her to come down, she did. I thought that she would fold easily, but when she came outside she did not follow me. Instead, she cursed me. Such a small,

251

brittle girl – I did not expect it.'

'How did she curse you?' Ash asked when he did not go on.

He did not look at her when he said, 'She cursed me to fall in love with a human girl, because she believed that might cause me to understand why what I have done over the course of many hundreds of years is wrong.' His voice carried a tinge of bitterness. 'Her curse did not seem to work at first. I did not think she was powerful enough of a witch to make the curse stick; whatever magic she had in her was tiny, compared to what I could hold in my hand. After all, I have lived for centuries, and she was nothing but a girl.'

'Why are you telling me this?' Ash asked.

He said softly, 'She was your mother.' When their eyes met, she saw that he looked at her with something like pain. 'And the first time I saw you, I knew that her curse would hold. But I do not think she knew that her daughter would be the girl caught in her spell.'

After everything that had happened that night, his words sank like stones in a still pond. She felt numb; this last revelation was too much, right now, to absorb. Finally she asked, 'Is it such a bad curse?'

'It is agony,' said Sidhean.

'It is not real,' she protested.

'It is as real as I am,' he claimed. And then he lifted her up out of her chair and he was holding her hands in his as they stood together, and she felt him press her hands to his chest, where his heartbeat thudded insistently against her fingertips. She would not look up at him, and because he was taller than her by a head, she found herself staring stubbornly at the embroidery on his waistcoat — it was a pattern of leaves and vines and perhaps roses in silver thread on silk of pearl grey, finer than any cloth she had ever seen. She had never been aware of such detail before: Had he never worn anything so beautiful? Or had she simply never opened her eyes? They stood together for what seemed to be an hour, or several, and she wondered if the world were spinning around her, for she felt dizzy. When he let her go she stumbled and nearly fell, but she caught herself on the edge of the chair and sat down again, hard, breathless.

'Something has changed within you,' he said accusingly.

She could not deny it.

But the force of him was still all around her and she could not see clearly. He drew a deep breath and said, 'You are not ready. Do not return here until you are, but do not delay for too long. I will not wait much longer.'

His words lifted her up from her seat, and at the edge of the clearing the moonlight path still floated. His face was turned away from her, and though she wanted to go to him, she could not. Her legs moved her against her will down the path, and then she was running through the Wood, crashing over the undergrowth and sending up waves of fairy light as she fled. She could not stop herself, even as she stumbled over tree roots, but at last she broke free of the Wood and began to cross the meadow. The pushing at her back was less intense now, but she could still feel it – as if there were hands on her shoulders, pressing her forward – and it directed her back through the kitchen garden and down the steps into the cellar. She pulled the door shut, and then a great, whistling wind came and shot the bolt home.

At first she stood, bewildered, in the dark. But as reality crept back into her consciousness – the chill of the cellar, the smell of it – she felt her way back to the trunks against the far wall. She unlatched one and fumbled around inside until she found something that would substitute for a blanket. Feeling drained, she lay down on the hard-packed dirt floor, and she slept.

She dreamed that she was running through the tallest, darkest trees of the Wood, her feet slamming into the uneven ground as she raced toward her goal. At last the trees parted and she found herself by the hawthorn tree in Rook Hill, and there was the grave of her mother, and beside the grave a young girl sat all in white, reading a book of fairy tales.

When Ash crashed into the clearing the girl turned to look up at her, and Ash saw that the girl's eyes were empty, and her skin was so pale it looked as if she were dead, and when the girl's mouth opened no words came out but Ash knew she was saying her name: *Aisling*. Ash backed away from the ghost girl, but the girl stood up and came towards her, her hands outstretched, and mouthed her name again. Ash did not know what to do, for she recognized the dress the girl was wearing – it was her work dress that she had worn while cleaning the parlour the other day – and that meant the girl must be herself. But the girl looked like a spectre, and if she were Ash, then Ash knew she had died as well.

She tried to run away, but she tripped on the root of the hawthorn tree and fell onto the grave, and the earth was heaving and warm beneath her, a monster rising out of the dark, and Ash wept, for she wanted to live.

19

Her stepmother did not release her from the cellar until midday. After she had awakened from that dream, she had tried to keep her eyes open, afraid of what other dreams might come. But as the crack of light around the cellar door brightened she nodded off into an uneasy doze. When the door finally opened it was noonday light that poured inside, and Ash put a hand over her eyes to block the sudden glare. Her stepmother said, 'You've slept enough. Get to work. And change out of that ridiculous dress.'

The fairy gown had not vanished in the course of the night, but in the light of day, it seemed to have faded. The crystal beads looked like paste now, and where Ana had torn the bodice, ordinary threads hung loose. In her room, Ash saw that the lid of her trunk was open, and inside where she had kept the fairy cloak and her books, there was nothing but her old work dress. She ran out through the kitchen after her stepmother, who was about to go upstairs, and demanded, 'What have you done with my things?'

Her stepmother paused on the bottom step, her lip curled. 'You stole from me, Aisling. Did you think I would not search your room to see what else you might have taken?'

'I did not steal from you,' Ash said angrily.

'You are a liar,' her stepmother said coldly.

'Where did you put my things?' Ash asked again.

'Goodness, it's as if you did have something valuable in there,' her stepmother said. 'If you still want those musty old books, you're too late – I burned them.' At the stricken look on Ash's face, her stepmother smiled and then continued up the stairs.

Feeling defeated, Ash went back into the kitchen, where she saw the cracked mirror on the table. She went to throw it away, but caught sight of her reflection in it. She looked a mess. Her hair, which she had remembered as being comical, looked like something out of a nightmare, especially with the bruise that had risen across her cheek and the dried blood on the corner of her mouth. She propped up the broken bits of mirror against a bowl, dampened a cloth in some water, and dabbed it against the cut. Then she picked up the kitchen shears that her stepmother had left on the table and clipped away the uneven ends of her hair. When she was finished, she combed out the inches that were left and stared at her unfamiliar reflection in the jagged pieces of glass. She noticed, for the first time, a light sprinkle of freckles on her cheeks, and she touched them in wonder. Had they always been there? Instead of throwing away the fragments of the mirror as she had planned, she folded them into an old rag and put the rag into the empty trunk.

As she stood up and went to the door, she saw a glimmer of silver out of the corner of her eye, and on the hook behind the door, the fairy cloak was hanging. It was as pristine and gleaming as the day she received it. She reached out to touch it, and saw the moonstone ring still on her hand. *Do not delay for too long*, Sidhean had said. As if the mere thought of him had set it off, she felt the ring begin to pulse like a living thing. For the first time, it made her angry. He had also told her not to come back until she was ready. Well, she was *not* ready. Until that day, Ash resolved that she would not wear this ring that chained her to him.

She wrenched it off, stuffing it into the cloak's interior pocket – but the pocket was not empty. Her fingers brushed against a book, and when she pulled it out she saw the faded fabric cover of her mother's herbal. She felt a surge of relief as she opened it to read her mother's handwriting, neat and measured, on the yellowed pages. She could not remember putting it in the cloak pocket, although at one time she had carried it with her like a good luck charm. She wanted to believe that she had left it there and forgotten about it – not that it had been placed there by any fairy magic.

Deliberately turning away from the cloak, she laid the herbal in her trunk beside the broken mirror, and she did her best to ignore the phantom presence of the moonstone ring on her hand.

Over the next several weeks, her stepmother did not allow her to leave the house unsupervised. She had to bring Clara with her on marketing days, but though her stepsister now controlled the purse, she did little else to restrict her. She spent much of their time together stealing sideways glances at her, as if Ash had become some sort of strange creature or, perhaps, an invalid. Once, as they were walking home from the village, Clara asked her, 'Where did you get those jewels, Ash? Did you really steal them?'

'Of course not,' Ash said.

'Then where did they come from? Did Ana tell you that by the next day they were nothing but paste? I thought they were diamonds, the night before.'

'They were never diamonds,' Ash said, though she did not know if that were true. Her younger stepsister paused and gave her a sceptical look, but she did not ask again.

As Yule approached, Ash went with her stepsisters while they were fitted for their new gowns: an emerald green one for Ana, a light blue one for Clara – who had yearned for a new gown for years. Neither of them spoke of the prince in Ash's company, though once when Ash was approaching the seamstress's dressing room, she heard Ana say, 'All anyone wants to know is who that woman was – apparently the prince keeps asking after her, but nobody knows her.' When Ash appeared in the doorway with the extra ribbon they had requested, Ana gave her a chilly look and did not speak of it again.

At night, before she fell asleep, her thoughts went in circles. At first, she had thought that with each passing day, she would come closer to accepting the fate that she had asked for. Perhaps she would remember how she had once wanted to trade her life away for an eternity she could not imagine. But she discovered that the opposite was happening: With each passing day, she wanted more time. This life that she had once hated no longer seemed so bleak. Her stepmother's words did little to upset her anymore. And more than anything, she wanted to see Kaisa again. But how long could she delay going back to Sidhean? Would he become angry? She began to wonder if any humans had ever managed to disentangle themselves from a fairy contract. None of the tales she had read gave her reason to hope; even Eilis, who had succeeded in her quest, fulfilled her end of the bargain.

She could not find a way out of the trap she had set for herself, and she was closer to despair than she had been since her mother died. She felt that the curse that Sidhean said her mother had lain on him might be the key to it all, so she took her mother's herbal out and re-read the faded handwriting by candlelight, but it only raised more questions. The only section that seemed to be remotely related to magic was the recipe to reverse a glamour, but it was not clear if the curse were a glamour at all. Sidhean had said that what he felt for her was as real as she was, and from what she recalled from the fairy tales, a glamour was only an illusion. If his love was real, it could not be a glamour.

She kept coming back to the pages her mother had written about love, but they were confusing. The notes on various herbs and plants seemed to be more informational than prescriptive, and there was no clear-cut recipe for a love spell or its reversal. There were notes on the weather – 'wait until the spring equinox has passed and the first rain has come and gone' – and there were notes she could only guess about: 'To charge someone with love is a great responsibility; there will be an equal yet unexpected reaction.' And then, at the end, was that sentence her mother had underlined: 'The knowledge will change him.' She did not know if her mother was referring to Sidhean, but she rolled the sentence around in her mind while she did her errands during her stepsisters' fittings.

One afternoon, her head spinning with these thoughts, she passed the church on her way back to the seamstress, and the black iron gate to the cemetery was hanging open. Ash began to pull it shut, the hinges squeaking, and the bottom of the gate dragged against the ground until it lodged in place, still partly open. She tugged on it but it wouldn't close, so she pushed it open again to free it, and then it seemed the most natural thing in the world to enter the yard. The browning grass had recently been clipped short, and the brick path leading to the graveyard was swept clean. She walked down the path and hesitated in front of the small, neat cemetery. There were still only a dozen or so headstones; few had been added since her father's funeral.

Ash went to the row farthest from the church, and there on the third tombstone she found her father's name. She remembered, from her childhood in Rook Hill, visiting her grandparents' graves in the family plot behind her mother's old home. Her mother had been the last in her family, so it was usually only the two of them who visited the graves on Souls Night, for her father was often away on business. Her mother would clean off the headstones with an old cloth and burn sage in a shallow pewter dish. She always left a loaf of bread on the ground when they departed, and sometimes, if they had them to spare, a bowl of red apples. They would sit on the ground among the old headstones and wait until the sage had burned away, and Ash still remembered the way she would fidget after only a few moments of stillness. Her mother would say to her gently, 'You only visit once a year, Ash. Sit still and give them a chance to see you.'

Ash ran her fingers over her father's name, and they came away covered with dust. She looked at the other gravestones, and some of them had been cleaned; some even had the burnt remnants of incense or herbs on the ground before them. Lady Isobel's prohibition of the old ways had not, Ash realized, been followed by everyone. She had not visited the grave since the day of her father's funeral, though she had passed the cemetery countless times since then. She looked up at the sky, and the blue-grey clouds were like bruises above her. She did not know how many days she had left here. She knelt down on the cold ground in front of the tombstone. The least she could do was sit still.

The weeks passed, and there was no sign of Sidhean, at least in her waking hours. Sometimes she dreamed of him: He would be walking down a long, moonlit hall, or he would be sitting in that clearing with the crystal fountain, but she could never see his face. She knew that he was waiting for her, and he was growing impatient. Sometimes she dreamed that she was walking in the Wood, passing the same stand of pine trees repeatedly; she would grow increasingly frustrated until she woke herself up, her hands balled into fists. Once she dreamed that she and Kaisa were lying on a blanket by the river, the sun warm on her hair, and they were laughing. She did not want to wake up from that dream, and when she did she turned her face into the pillow, yearning to spend one more moment in that summer afternoon. But it was winter, and outside the dawn was cold.

At supper, a fortnight before Yule, Lady Isobel informed Ash that she would be going with them into the City again, to spend the week at her sister's house. 'But you will not be attending any of the celebrations,' her stepmother said. 'I've told my sister that you're not allowed to leave the house and that her housekeeper is to keep an eye on you to make sure you don't steal anything.' Ash poured her stepmother more wine and did not answer. 'Did you hear me, Aisling?' her stepmother said.

'Of course,' Ash said.

'And you will speak with respect to me and your stepsisters,' Lady Isobel said sternly. 'Don't think that your brief taste of civilized life means that you're worth anything more than a life below stairs.'

Her stepmother's words washed over her; Ash barely heard them. She was thinking of one thing only: At Yule, she could see Kaisa – perhaps for the last time.

20

This year, there was no sign of the Royal Hunt as they drove from West Riding to the City, though every time Ash saw a rider on the horizon, she held her breath until they were close enough for her to see that it was not the King's Huntress. In the City, the palace winked at them between buildings as they drove towards the Page Street mansion. Once again Ash shared Gwen's small attic room, and that night as Gwen lay asleep in bed, Ash lay awake, thinking.

Gwen was engaged, now, to a butcher's son. Colin had left the household and gone south to find his luck in the trades, Gwen had told her before she went to sleep that night. 'I never liked him that much anyway,' Gwen whispered. 'Peter is so wonderful to me, I can't believe I would ever have wanted anyone else.' She beamed, and Ash envied her. 'You must let me introduce you to him tomorrow night when we go to the Square for the bonfire.'

'I am not allowed to go,' Ash said, hanging her spare

dress on a hook behind Gwen's door.

'I heard about that,' Gwen said. 'But no one will care if you go; you know we all detest Lady Isobel, don't you?'

'Really?'

'Of course,' Gwen answered. 'She's horrible to us when she visits, and her daughter Ana isn't much better. It's no wonder she can't find a husband.' Gwen climbed into bed and continued, 'I hope for your sake, though, that she does soon. At least then you won't have to deal with her any more.'

'One can only hope,' Ash said grimly. She got into bed as well, but she couldn't sleep, and after lying uncomfortably still for too long, she decided it was better to leave Gwen in peace.

Downstairs in the kitchen the fire was banked, but when she knelt down on the hearth, the stones were still warm. She held her hands out to the embers for a moment and then sat down, leaning against the chimney. She wondered whether it was snowing in the Wood. It had begun to snow shortly after they arrived in the City that afternoon, and already the ground was thinly blanketed in white. It would be a cold night in the Wood, but in the morning the tracks of the deer would be clear and sharp, and it would be child's play to uncover them. She fell in and out of a fitful sleep, dreaming of the Wood and the clean, unbroken snow beneath her feet. She thought she saw a doe, her huge, glossy eyes peeking out from behind an evergreen, but then it was only the vanishing tail of a bounding rabbit, leaving long, trailing pawprints in the snow. She thought she smelled the scent of pine burning: a spicy, woodsy scent from a campfire. But then she heard the cook's voice saying, 'Goodness, it's you again – you never change, do you? Get upstairs and get dressed; it's time to serve the ladies breakfast.'

Ash opened her eyes, blinking in the morning light, and saw the cook looking at her with her hands on her hips. 'I'm sorry,' Ash began, but the cook interrupted her.

'I'm sure I don't know why you prefer to sleep on the floor rather than in a nice bed, but it doesn't matter. Hurry up and get ready; Lady Isobel won't be kept waiting.'

That entire day as she attended to Ana's and Clara's demands, she felt as if she were only partially there. She worked methodically, but her mind wandered to Sidhean, to Kaisa, to the last time she had seen her, the fairy gown on her skin like a live creature. She helped Ana dress, lacing her into the tight bodice until her stepsister gasped for breath; she braided Ana's hair with green ribbons and strung an ornate gold choker around her neck; she listened with a carefully blank expression on her face as Ana complained about the fit and cut and drape of the gown. Every hour that passed brought her closer to the moment when she would see Kaisa. She helped her stepsisters and stepmother into their elaborate fur cloaks after they had dined with their cousins on a light meal, and she stood on the front step with the other servants as their hired carriages came to take them to the palace. And when Gwen snaked her arm into hers and whispered, 'Come upstairs and get dressed – you are coming with us tonight,' she did not object. She knew that the King's Huntress would come to the City Square that night, as tradition demanded.

But as Gwen put on her costume – 'I am going to be a rich merchant,' she said – Ash only sat quietly in the window. 'Do you want me to find you something to wear?' Gwen asked, looking at Ash in the mirror, but Ash shook her head.

'No, thank you,' she said. 'Don't go to the trouble.'

'But you cannot go to the Square in your work dress,' Gwen objected, turning to look at her.

So Ash took out the fairy cloak, which she had impulsively brought with her, and watched Gwen's eyes widen as the silvery length of it spread out on her bed. 'I will wear this,' said Ash, 'and no one will know that I am only wearing my servant's dress underneath.' When she put it on, she reached into the interior pocket and felt the moonstone ring there. But instead of sliding it onto her finger, she transferred it to the pocket of her dress, where she could feel it against her hip. He knew that she was coming.

Despite Lady Isobel's command that Ash remain at the house, none of the servants seemed inclined to enforce her directions, and they happily exclaimed at Ash's fine cloak and made room for her in the wagon that they took to the City Square. When they arrived, Ash followed them into the centre of the Square where hundreds of people were gathered around a huge bonfire; the smoke of it rose like the breath of a great dragon. North of the Square she could see the white spires of the palace lit up for the ball that was to take place that night, and all around her the voices of the revellers rang out like bells. Ash wondered who Prince Aidan would choose as his bride that night, and she wondered how disappointed her stepsisters would be when it was not one of them.

She let Gwen pull her into the ring of dancers circling the bonfire, and as they whirled around to the sound of drums and pipes, each step she took brought her closer to the raucous, joyful merriment of that night. Slowly, the dazed feeling that had hung like a cloud around her for weeks began to clear away. At last she could feel the hard stones of the Square beneath her feet, the fabric of her dress as it swung around her legs, the heat from the bonfire on her cheeks. As the people swayed and stamped and sung their way around the bonfire, Ash knew that this was what the fairies were always hunting for: a circle of joy, hot and brilliant, the scent of love in the deepest winter. But all they could do was create a pale, crystalline imitation, perfect and cold. How it must disappoint them: that they would never be human.

When the Royal Hunt arrived with their purses full of gold, she watched them circle the Square and then fling out sparkling coins to the cheering revellers. She saw Kaisa on her bay mare, her black velvet cloak fluttering behind her as she rode; but instead of dismounting to join the revellers, the hunt soon rode out of the Square and continued on towards the palace. 'Why are they not staying?' Ash asked Gwen anxiously.

'Tonight the prince is to announce the name of his bride,' Gwen said. 'You know that, don't you? They are going to the ball, of course.'

Ash looked at Gwen and at the revellers dancing around the bonfire, and the flickering flames cast all their faces in gold. She felt the time left to her dwindling away, but she was resolved: She must go to Kaisa. Without saying a word, she turned away from Gwen and began to walk towards the edge of the Square. She did not look back when Gwen called after her, and as soon as she broke free of the crowd, she quickened her pace so that she would not lose her nerve.

The streets were empty that night, and above her the sky was clear. She could see the stars, sharp and bright, and the half-moon glowed in the east. The palace had not seemed far away, but it was situated high on the crest of a hill, and she had to walk up streets that grew steeper and steeper as she drew closer to it. On the last stretch of avenue that led up to the main gates, carriages lined the roadway, and footmen and drivers were standing about on the side of the road, laughing and talking to each other. Several of them turned to watch her as she walked past them, and one asked if she were late to the ball, but she did not answer. When she reached the iron gates to the palace grounds, the guards asked for her invitation, and she said, 'Is not every eligible woman invited? You must let me through.'

The guards looked at each other, and the older one said gruffly, 'Go on. You're late as it is.'

She continued up the avenue towards the palace, past the courtyard where her fairy carriage had deposited her on Souls Night, through the gilded gates and into the great hall to the entrance of the ballroom. She stood just inside the entryway and looked out over the sea of dancers. She saw women in violet silk and burgundy satin, with their golden and black and auburn hair bound in jewels or ribbons, and she saw men dressed in black and sapphire and green velvet. On the dais on the right side of the ballroom the King and Queen were enthroned, and at the King's right hand was the King's Huntress. Ash took a deep breath and began to walk across the ballroom, pushing through the revelers as best she could. It was like picking her way through the wildest part of the Wood in the dark, for people stood in her way and stared at her as she tried to pass them. Though she was wearing the fairy cloak, she wore no jewels, and her hair was inelegantly short. They did not know if she were a lost servant or an unwelcome interloper. She did not know if she could actually do what she had decided to do, for it seemed reckless — as reckless, she guessed, as Sidhean had said she was.

By the time she reached the dais, those who were seated at the King's table had seen her approaching, for her path across the ballroom had not been smooth. As she went up the steps, a servant came to block her way, and she thought she must surely have looked a bit crazed, but she said, 'Please, I am here to see the huntress.' And there, before her, was Kaisa, who had recognized her as she made her way to the dais.

'Let her pass,' she said to the servant, who looked dubious but backed away as instructed. Kaisa looked at Ash, standing several steps below her, and said uncertainly, 'Ash? Are you all right?'

With her heart hammering in her throat, Ash asked, 'Will you do me the honour of dancing with me?' She looked up at Kaisa, and the huntress's look of bewilderment was changing, slowly, to a small, tentative smile. It steadied Ash, and she extended her hand across the distance.

Kaisa came down the steps, took her hand, and said, 'Yes.'

Ash felt as if her whole being had come to rest in her fingertips where they touched Kaisa's hand, and it did not matter that several of the revellers had come towards the dais and were watching them, their mouths open, for this was one of the more unusual things ever to happen at a Yule ball. She and Kaisa turned down the steps to go back to the dance floor, and when her fairy cloak became tangled around her legs, she unclasped it with her free hand and let it fall onto the steps. The music had stopped when she was making her way up the dais, but now as they stood facing each other on the dance floor, the musicians began playing again, and Ash said, slightly horrified, 'I do not know how to dance.' She was wearing only her ordinary shoes now, and she suspected that they would not be as skilled as those fairy slippers that had saved her on Souls Night.

Kaisa broke into laughter, and it was a good, solid laugh, and soon enough Ash could not help but laugh with her. When they had recovered enough to look around them, Kaisa said, 'It is only a pavane. Come, the steps are simple.' The couples had recommenced the dance when it had appeared that the huntress and her mysterious guest were too consumed with laughter to join them, but it was easy enough to link their arms together and slip into the procession. They passed Prince Aidan, who was dancing with a woman who was decidedly neither of Ash's stepsisters, and he smiled at them as they went by. Ash thought she might have seen her stepmother through the crowd, her face white with surprise, but then they reached the end of the processional and Kaisa said, 'Come, we can leave the ball behind for a moment.'

She led Ash towards the doors to the garden, but instead of going outside they went through a doorway into a servants' corridor, where waiters were rushing by with flagons of wine. Though they looked at them curiously, Kaisa paid no attention, and took Ash through a swinging wooden door into a deserted antechamber. The floor was inlaid with polished wood in the shape of a star, and above them a wrought iron chandelier held a dozen burning candles. Huge tapestries depicting landscapes hung on three walls: green farming valleys, the wild coast of the sea, and the Wood. 'Where are we?' Ash asked.

'That is the throne room,' Kaisa said, pointing to the closed double doors in the fourth wall.

Ash realized that she was still holding the huntress's hand, and she became suddenly self-conscious. 'I think I made a scene,' she said apologetically. Kaisa burst into laughter again, and Ash laughed, too, for it did seem quite funny. As their laughter died, Kaisa pulled her closer. She twined her fingers in Ash's hair – 'This is something new,' she murmured – and kissed her. Ash felt her entire body move towards her, as if every aspect of her being was reorienting itself to this woman, and they could not be close enough.

She became aware of the other feeling gradually, for it was swimming against the current within her: Sidhean's pain and sorrow, rising up like a beast, and it pushed itself between the two of them. Ash put her hands on Kaisa's shoulders and pushed back, gasping for breath. 'I am sorry,' Ash said miserably, tears filling her eyes.

'What is it?' Kaisa asked, and looked at her with much tenderness.

Ash took Kaisa's hands in hers and looked down, unable to meet her eyes. The cuffs of Kaisa's black sleeves were embroidered with gold serpents, and their eyes glittered with tiny red garnets. She said in an unsteady voice, 'I came here so that I might see you before . . . before I go. I must go and settle my debt.'

Kaisa lifted her right hand to brush a strand of Ash's hair behind her ear, and she cupped her cheek in her palm. 'What is your debt?' she asked softly.

'It is my own, and no other's,' Ash said. In her mind's eye she saw Sidhean pacing by the crystal fountain, and she felt pity for him, for now she knew what it was to be in love.

The realization hit her hard, and she was stunned by it. A memory flooded into her: She was at her mother's grave, and she heard her mother's voice in her ear. *There will come a change, and you will know what to do.* The knowledge of love had changed her. It focussed what had once been a blur; it turned her world around and presented her with a new landscape. Now, she would do anything to bring Kaisa happiness. And if the knowledge of love could change her, would it not also change Sidhean? She began to think that there might be a way out, after all.

She raised her eyes to look at the huntress, and Kaisa's eyes were wet with tears.

'Are you coming back?' Kaisa asked.

'I hope so,' Ash said. She stepped away from her, gently, and then turned to go. She did not let herself look back.

In the ballroom, dancer after dancer gaped at her as she fled. At last she passed into the great hall and then was outside, where the night air was cold against her flushed skin. She realized that she had left her cloak somewhere in the ballroom, but she could not go back. She left the palace grounds and continued down the sloping avenue, and when she neared the sounds of the crowd in the City Square, she went on.

By the time she reached the City gates, she had become numb to the cold, though the road was covered in a thin layer of snow and her breath steamed into the chilly air. The moon was overhead by now, and as she walked she watched it slowly descend toward the west. She did not know how long she walked – time seemed to be compressed, as it was when she had walked to Rook Hill. She felt almost frozen when she at last reached West Riding, but she did not stop at Quinn House even though her teeth chattered from the cold. She hunted for the path at the edge of the Wood, but the snow had obscured all traces of it. Finally she entered the forest near the main hunting road, but after going only a few feet the trail disappeared. She did not know which way to turn, and the freshly fallen snow had erased all the familiar landmarks. So she simply chose a direction, picking her way around tree roots and snowdrifts, until finally she came to a small clearing where the snow had not fallen. In the centre was a crystal fountain, and when she saw it, water sprang from the leaves of a diamond hawthorn tree. Just beyond the crystal fountain there was a small round table and two familiar chairs. She heard a step behind her and turned to see that Sidhean was standing in the dark between the trees, where he had been waiting for her.

'You are nearly frozen,' said Sidhean, and he took the cloak he was wearing and placed it around her shoulders. He put his arms around her, and her feet and hands burned with pain as she slowly warmed up. As they stood together, she began to hear the steady rhythm of his heartbeat, and her breathing slowed to match his, until she felt as though they were nearly one being.

Dragging herself away from him took every ounce of

courage she had, and when at last she was free and had put a hand's breadth of cold night air between them, she looked up at his shadowed eyes and said, 'Sidhean, for many years, you have been my only friend, though such a friendship is by definition a queer one, for your people and mine are not meant to love one another. But you said that you have been cursed to love me, and I have realized that if the curse is strong – and if you truly love me – then you will set me free.' She paused, drawing a ragged breath, and took the moonstone ring out of her pocket and put it into the palm of his hand. She said: 'It will end here tonight. I will be yours for this one night, and then the curse shall be broken.'

'One night in my world is not the same as one night in yours.'

'But morning always comes,' she said.

He stood in silence for a long moment, but at last he bowed his head. 'Very well. It will end here tonight.' She saw him, then, as clearly as she might ever see him. He was more powerful and more seductive than any human she would ever know, but faced with her, he would do her bidding. She felt as though she were a lion uncurling from a long nap, and she wanted to flex her claws.

All around them the Wood was changing, shifting, as if a veil were being lifted and she was finally allowed to see what was behind it. He stepped back and extended his hand to her.

She asked, 'Will I die?'

He answered, 'Only a little,' and she put her hand in his, and she felt the ring between their palms, burning like a brand.

21

When she awoke, the midmorning sun was slanting into the clearing where she lay on the ground. Above her the trees were in full leaf, and the air was as warm as midsummer. She stretched lazily and blinked against the clear golden light, feeling as though she had slept so well she might never have to sleep again. With a yawn she sat up and saw that a low table nearby was set with breakfast for one. She ate sweet bread and segments of orange and ripe cherries, and drank a light, warm tea that invigorated her. As she set down the teacup she noticed something on her right hand, and she turned her palm up to the sunlight and saw a pale, circular scar. She blinked slowly, for her memory was strangely blurred. She closed her eyes briefly, and beneath the scent of growing things was the faintest perfume of jasmine. She remembered, for one fleeting moment, a hunt dressed all in white; a garden of lushly blooming roses; Sidhean beside her. When she opened her eyes again, the table had vanished. She knew that when she left this place, she would never see it again.

There was a small path at the edge of the clearing, and scarcely three steps into the Wood, the winter returned. When she looked back at where she had been, there was only the cold morning behind her. But as the sun filtered down through the bare branches and glittered on the new snow, the Wood was every bit as alive as it was in the summer. Her footprints pushed aside the snow to reveal the deep brown of fallen leaves, and red chokecherries climbed among the evergreens – startling colour in the grey-and-white landscape. She soon came to a clearly marked trail dotted with the hoofprints of deer; it took her to the treeline and, finally, the meadow behind Quinn House. She could not see her footprints from the night before; the whole of the meadow was clean and unbroken. She walked across the open space, her feet crunching through the snow into the dry grass below.

She let herself in through the garden gate and the kitchen door. It was silent and chilly indoors, and it no longer felt like home. She went into her room and opened the trunk, and there at the bottom were her books of fairy tales, her mother's herbal, and the medallion – Sidhean's final gift to her. She thought she might put it on a chain, one day, and it would remind her of the fairy who had, in his own strange way, shown her how to save herself. She put the books and the medallion into a canvas bag, then went out into the front hall and took down one of Clara's spare cloaks. Before she left, she paused with her hand on the front door and looked back at the hall for a minute. The door to the kitchen was partway open, and she could see the edge of the kitchen table and the handle of a mug. Then she opened the front door and stepped outside, and the sun was bright in her eyes.

Just past West Riding, as she was walking up the same road she had taken the night before, she heard a merchant's wagon coming behind her. When she waved at the driver, he halted beside her and asked, 'Where are you going?'

'To the City,' she replied. 'Are you headed there?'

'I am,' he said. 'There's room for you in the back, if you'd like.' He gestured toward the wagon bed, which was piled with bolts of cloth. She thanked him and climbed on and watched as the village of West Riding receded behind them. When they arrived in the City, the merchant dropped her off at the Square, where a dozen men and women were cleaning up the remains of the bonfire from the night before. As she passed them, she saw a glint of gold in a crack between the paving stones, and she bent down to pick up a gold coin, stamped on one side with a crown and on the other with a stag's head. She pocketed it and continued walking.

By the time she arrived at Page Street, it was nearly

noon. She hesitated on the street in front of Lady Isobel's sister's house, and decided to slip around the rear to the servants' entrance. In the yard, one of the stable hands saw her, but she merely waved at him and went on to the back door. Inside she nearly managed to slip up the back stairs unseen, but the cook spied her from the kitchen and cried, 'Aisling! Whatever are you doing? We were certain you had run away.'

Ash paused on the bottom step and said, 'I'm only here to pick up my things, and then I am going. Please don't tell anyone.' But the cook's expression did not convince her that she would keep quiet, so Ash ran up the stairs to Gwen's room, not waiting for a response. Gwen was not upstairs, but the room had been torn apart in her absence – Gwen's clothes were flung everywhere. She had to search through the mess to find her things, and when she stood up to leave, Clara was standing in the doorway.

'I heard you come in,' Clara said. 'Where have you been?' She eyed what Ash was wearing and asked, 'Is that my cloak?'

'Yes,' Ash said, and took it off and handed it to her. 'I had to borrow it.'

'Did you go home?' Clara asked curiously.

'Yes.'

'Mother will never take you back, now,' Clara said.

Ash let out a laugh. 'I don't intend to come back.'

'That was you, then, last night with the King's

Huntress?' Clara said.

Last night seemed an eternity ago, and Ash wondered just how long she had been with Sidhean. But she put all thoughts of him aside, for today was the day after Yule, and she answered, 'Yes, that was me.'

'I thought so, but Mother and Ana would not believe it,' Clara said. She grinned mischievously. 'You have outmatched Lord Rowan.'

Ash smiled, and she asked, 'Who, then, did Prince Aidan choose?'

'He chose an heiress from Seatown – I do not even know her name.'

Her stepsister sounded carefully nonchalant about it, and Ash did not press her for further details. She slung her satchel over her shoulder and said, 'I must go. Take care of yourself – and don't listen to them.' Clara broke into a smile, and on impulse Ash went to her stepsister and embraced her.

When they parted, Clara looked surprised. 'Good luck, Ash,' she said.

'Good luck to you, too,' Ash replied, and then she went quickly down the stairs and out the kitchen door, ignoring the cook's questions. Outside, she began walking away and did not look back, though just before she reached the end of the street she heard her stepmother shouting her name. She went up the hills again, retracing her steps from the night before, but this morning there were no carriages parked by the side of the road, and the thin blanket of snow was melting, making the cobblestones slippery beneath her feet. At the palace gates, the guards were tending to a line of wagons waiting to enter the grounds, and they did not notice when she slipped between the wagons and into the outer courtyard.

For the first time she noticed that in the centre of the courtyard was a fountain from which a horse and rider reared, and water plumed out from the horse's mouth. Ahead of her, the heavy wooden doors to the palace were closed, but a smaller door set within them was unbarred, and she went to the door and pushed it open. Inside, the great hall was lit only by light from the tall, narrow windows set high in the wall, and there were servants polishing the wide expanse of marble. They looked in her direction when she entered, and one said to her, 'The servants' entrance is to the left of the courtyard; you've come in the wrong way.'

'I'm sorry,' she said. 'Which way should I go?'

'Don't bother – just take the corridor down at the end of the hall and go downstairs,' he told her. She nodded and went in the direction he pointed, but instead of taking the stairs she went down a different corridor, walking quickly so that no one would think she did not know where she was going. She passed a tall span of glass windows that overlooked a sunny courtyard; she passed the balcony on which she had stood with the huntress. At last the corridor narrowed and became a wood-panelled hallway that seemed more like someone's home than a palace, hung with portraits of huntresses dressed in green and brown. She came to the circular chamber inlaid with the image of the stag, and she went to the black doors in the far wall and knocked on them. She waited for what seemed like hours, and just as she was raising her hand to knock once again, the door was opened by a servant wearing the King's livery.

'I am here to see Kaisa,' she said.

The servant answered, 'She is not here.'

'Where is she?' Ash asked. 'I must see her.'

He was staring at her as if puzzled, and then she saw recognition dawn on his face. 'You are the woman from last night,' he said, looking at her with interest.

'Please,' she said, 'just tell me where she is.'

Something in her tone softened him, and he said at last, 'She is in the stables.'

'Thank you,' Ash said gratefully, and turned back the way she came. When she returned to the great hall she asked a servant there how to find the stables, and she saw that he recognized her as well. She began to wonder how many people had seen her flee the ballroom. He told her to go back into the courtyard and follow the gravel path around the perimeter; it disappeared through a high stone archway that opened into another, smaller courtyard. On the far side, a set of wide wooden doors gaped open. Beyond them was the stable yard, with stalls opening onto the yard on three sides. She walked slowly past the stalls on her left, looking in each one, and though the horses raised their eyes to her, she did not see the huntress. Just then a stable hand came out of a stall pushing a handcart, and when he saw her he called out, 'Are you looking for someone?' But she did not answer, for in the corner stall, where a bay mare stood contentedly eating her noonday feed, Ash found the person she was looking for.

Kaisa was brushing the horse, and when she heard Ash's footsteps, she looked up from her work, and her hand stilled. She looked tired, Ash saw, as if she had not slept well. There were purple shadows beneath her eyes, and there was a smudge of dirt on her cheek. She wore a black tunic that had seen better days, and old brown leggings tucked into scuffed work boots. Now that the moment had come, Ash felt unexpectedly shy, and all the words she had thought she might say abandoned her.

It was Kaisa who broke the silence. 'After you left last night, it was all anyone could talk about,' she said. 'They asked me about you, but all I could tell them was that I loved you, and I did not know when or if you would return.' By now Kaisa had put down the brush and had come to stand before her. 'They brought me your cloak,' she added, 'and I have kept it for you.'

Ash stepped toward her, dropping her satchel on the ground, and took the huntress's hands in her own. She felt as if the whole world could hear her heart beating as, she said, 'After I left last night, I was not sure whether I would be able to return, but I hoped so, and now I can tell you that it is finished, and I am free to love you.' Then they took the last step together, and when she kissed her, her mouth as warm as summer, the taste of her sweet and clear, she knew, at last, that she was home.

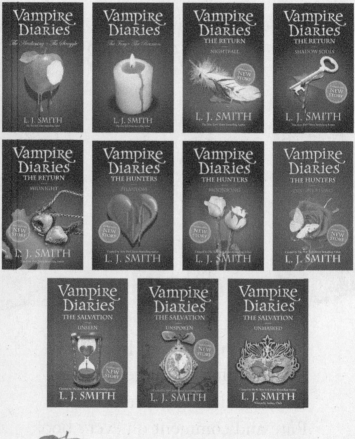

the Vampire Diaries

Stefan's Diaries

Stefan and Damon weren't always fighting or succumbing to their bloodlusts. Once they were loving siblings who enjoyed all the riches and happiness that their wealthy lifestyle afforded them; loyal brothers who happened to both fall for the same beautiful woman. Once they were alive...

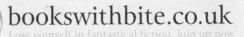

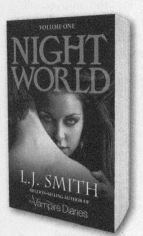